Sweet On You

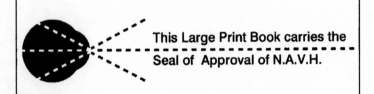

This Large Print Book carries the
Seal of Approval of N.A.V.H.

Sweet On You

Janet Wellington

Thorndike Press • Waterville, Maine

Published in 2006 by arrangement with Janet Wellington.

Thorndike Press® Large Print Romance.

The tree indicium is a trademark of Thorndike Press.

The text of this Large Print edition is unabridged.
Other aspects of the book may vary from the original edition.

Set in 16 pt. Plantin by Minnie B. Raven.

Printed in the United States on permanent paper.

Library of Congress Cataloging-in-Publication Data

Wellington, Janet.
    Sweet on you / by Janet Wellington. — Large print ed.
      p. cm. — (Thorndike Press large print romance)
    ISBN 0-7862-8262-2 (lg. print : hc : alk. paper)
    1. Large type books. I. Title. II. Thorndike Press
large print romance series.
PS3573.E463S94 2005
  813′.6—dc22   2005027327

To my mother, who taught me to love books, and to my dad, who always believed I would write one. A special thanks to author Cindy Van Rooy for her encouragement to have *Sweet On You* available in large print. To my young friend Brian Glasser, for his "World Famous (Maybe Not) Cookie" recipe. To author and teacher, Diane Pershing, for original inspiration. And, most importantly, to my own live-in hero, Jim, for his understanding of deadlines and writing schedules, and for his endless encouragement and patience. And to you, dear reader: always be ready to give true love a second chance.

As the Founder/CEO of NAVH, the only national health agency solely devoted to those who, although not totally blind, have an eye disease which could lead to serious visual impairment, I am pleased to recognize Thorndike Press* as one of the leading publishers in the large print field.

Founded in 1954 in San Francisco to prepare large print textbooks for partially seeing children, NAVH became the pioneer and standard setting agency in the preparation of large type.

Today, those publishers who meet our standards carry the prestigious "Seal of Approval" indicating high quality large print. We are delighted that Thorndike Press is one of the publishers whose titles meet these standards. We are also pleased to recognize the significant contribution Thorndike Press is making in this important and growing field.

Lorraine H. Marchi, L.H.D.
Founder/CEO
NAVH

* Thorndike Press encompasses the following imprints: Thorndike, Wheeler, Walker and Large Print Press.

One

"It's a lovely seventy degrees already in America's finest city. Charlie Chattham here, bringing you all your favorite golden oldies on a beautiful Monday morning in sunny San Diego —"

Gabe Freeman winced and lowered the volume of the radio. "Enjoy your last Monday morning broadcast, Charlie. May Los Angeles be everything you want it to be — I sure hope you know what you're giving up." He shook his head as he reached for the silver commuter mug, craving his must-have morning java.

He agreed with Charlie, though. It was a perfect morning in southern California. At the age of thirty-nine, Gabe had the ideal life, and it was getting better every day. Flipping off the air conditioning, he lowered the driver's side window. A moist ocean breeze filled his Volvo's interior space which suddenly felt much too cramped.

Everything was perfect — except for the

7

traffic. He wasn't used to the early morning backup on the Coronado Bridge. In fact, he wasn't used to even being awake before noon, let alone sitting in rush hour traffic. Since his promotion, Gabe had finally been given a reprieve from the graveyard shift and plunked into the prime a.m. drive time slot. He'd worked hard to get where he was and intended to enjoy every moment — as soon as he woke up enough.

A horn blared somewhere in the line of cars behind him, jarring his thoughts. He supposed he would get used to all this noise eventually.

"Traffic is just starting to back up this morning and the bridge is slowing down as you approach the toll plaza."

"No kidding." Gabe glanced in the rearview mirror at the car behind him. An attractive blonde was talking on a cell phone, her free hand periodically slapping the steering wheel.

Gabe shuddered as he watched her finish the call and immediately punch in another number. The reality of what people were like driving to work every morning was beginning to sink in. Even so, he was looking forward to the challenge of capturing their attention. He intended to distract them from obsessing about how much business they could get done on the way in to their jobs.

"And if you're listening out there, Gamblin' Gabe Freeman, you'd better be good to my faithful KGLD listeners or I'll have to leave Smogtown and come back here and kick your you-know-what."

Groaning, Gabe loosened his Armani tie and ran his fingers through his short brown curls. He glanced at himself in the mirror. The shorter style provided the *GQ* look he needed in his new position. Even though it was easier to deal with, he found he missed his previously shoulder-length hair.

Another horn blared. Today's commute was beginning to be an exercise in patience. Gabe's jaw tightened as he clenched his teeth. The traffic jam was going to make him late for his first advertising meeting at the station.

As he moved his car forward, Gabe was forced to stop abruptly. He reached for the white floral box on the seat next to him to prevent it from falling. The box was filled with long-stemmed red roses to commemorate the six months until his wedding to Jillian. Their wedding was planned for June. Right on schedule.

"Hey! You want to get your head out of

9

the clouds and move up a little?"

Blinking, Gabe realized there were now two car lengths between him and the car ahead of him. The grating voice of the beautiful blonde yelling out her window pulled him back to reality.

As Gabe pulled forward and eased to a stop, the line of bright blue tollbooths finally came into view. As more horns blared, he watched as a denim-clad arm swung out of a pickup in line ahead of him and flipped the bird to the impatient lines of traffic. The man then pointed ahead.

A poster sat on an easel near one of the tollbooths. Red and white heart-shaped balloons floated above the sign, bouncing in the light breeze.

Close enough now to read the poster, Gabe realized why his line was moving so slowly. In big black letters, the poster read:

STOP AND WISH CELESTE A
HAPPY 40TH BIRTHDAY!
SHE'S SINGLE AND DEFINITELY
NOT OVER THE HILL!

So that's why the line was so slow. Gabe sighed. Stuck in the birthday-girl line. He resigned himself to the fact that he would be walking in during the middle of his first important meeting, and not making the greatest impression on the rest of the day crew. At times like this it certainly helped to be engaged to the station owner's daughter.

As Gabe inched closer, he stared at the source of his troubles, watching the woman in the tollbooth with unexpected interest. His gaze was drawn first to her hair. Shoulder-length, it hung in wild, unruly waves and curls. Though brown in color, there were distinctive red highlights that caught the sun's rays every time she leaned out of the booth to collect a toll. The hair-style's effect was a little frenzied, though the color was dazzling — like morning flames in the morning sunlight.

As she leaned out of the booth, he could see she wore a silk, purple sleeveless blouse tucked into a bizarre-looking skirt. The skirt was actually made of dozens of silk ties that had been sewn together vertically so that each point formed the hem of the skirt. The effect was unique, almost bohemian.

"Happy birthday, Celeste!" a cheerful voice called out from a Jeep in an adjacent lane.

Gabe watched as Celeste pivoted, then smiled and waved at the driver. Sunlight

11

reflected off dozens of silver bangles on her arm and flashed painfully in Gabe's eyes. It took a moment to blink away the glare.

The beautiful blonde's horn blared again from behind. Gabe winced, shot the woman a glare in his rearview mirror and eased his car forward.

"We've got a listener's request up next. This one's just for you, lovely Linda-in-La-Mesa. And if you're supposed to be at work at the eight o'clock hour, you're already seventeen minutes late so you might as well just kick back and enjoy the —"

Gabe snapped off the radio in frustration. Maybe everyone else was running late too, he thought, biting at an uneven thumbnail.

His attention returned to the birthday girl. Without the facts the poster provided, it would have been difficult to guess her age at forty based on what he could see from three car lengths back. Perhaps it was her outfit. No, it was more her attitude, he thought. She had a youthful glow. Undoubtedly a free spirit who wouldn't understand the overheated tempers the unexpected delay was causing.

She probably flitted from job to job, Gabe thought, unable to picture her in the corporate world. She certainly wasn't the typical dress-for-success woman climbing the corporate ladder.

Gabe stared as Celeste flashed a broad grin at the car filled with teens singing "Happy Birthday" to her in boisterous, off-key voices. The smile she offered was radiant and candid, as if she was the kind of person who held nothing back. Unrestricted. Uninhibited.

A question of what she might be like in bed popped into Gabe's head. He blinked in surprise and shoved the vision away, mystified at the unexpected thought.

Her wild curls bounced as Celeste shook her head. She stood next to the car with her hands on her hips, waiting for the serenade to end. Gabe was unable to prevent his gaze from dropping to where her hands rested on the curves below her waist. She definitely wasn't thin, he concluded, but looked deliciously soft and feminine — so unlike the popular wafer-thin models his fiancée labored to emulate.

A horn blast followed by the staccato beeping of his own watch alarm brought Gabe instantly back to reality. Only one more car between him and the birthday girl.

As the car in front of him paid the dollar toll, Gabe glanced at the white box on the seat beside him. Impulsively, he loosened the lid and, without taking his eyes off Celeste, he reached in and pulled out one of the roses.

Celeste turned away from the flow of traffic, sneaking a look at the digital clock on the cash register as she deposited the toll. Fifty more minutes left on her shift and the embarrassing ordeal would be over.

Her cheeks ached from smiling and she longed to say her final yes-it's-really-my-birthday and get back home. Four hours of cheerfully enduring the steady stream of comments had been exhausting.

Celeste had spent the better part of the morning contemplating an appropriate payback for her friend Kay's good-natured antics. Perhaps introducing Kay's three young daughters to makeup and nail polish would do, she thought, smiling at the vision of Kay's youngsters with bright lilac eyeshadow and chili-pepper-red lipgloss.

It would serve her right. Celeste sighed, put on a forced smile and readied herself for the next birthday commentary.

As she turned and leaned out the opening in the booth, she extended her hand toward the driver of the next car. Instead of currency, a long-stemmed red rose was placed in the palm of her hand.

Her gaze locked on the perfect bloom, momentarily ignoring its presenter. Her fingers wrapped around the stem and she brought the unexpected offering to her lips, feeling the petal softness, breathing the intoxicating fragrance.

"I . . . I still intend to pay . . ."

Celeste returned her attention to the driver of the waiting car. "Pardon me?"

"Here's my money, I mean . . . the rose is just . . . for your birthday. The sign . . ."

The driver's words came out in an adolescent tumble as Celeste stared at him. Another yuppie ready to join the rat race, she thought. A drop-dead gorgeous one, though, and impeccably dressed. Pressed white long-sleeved shirt, lightly starched. Gold cufflinks. A nice touch. Expensive tie. Flawless taste in clothes in the current popular shades of olive. Obviously very image conscious. Probably an ambitious executive with a sassy little assistant who aimed to please, she thought.

"I bet it's been a tough morning for you."

Celeste blinked in surprise at the empathetic comment. It wasn't what she'd expected.

"Oh, not too bad," she said. "A little repetitious."

"So, who put up the poster?" he asked, nodding his head in the direction of the sign.

"An overly concerned neighbor of mine," she answered, "who thinks I'm lonely."

The driver nodded his understanding. "Have you been plotting your revenge, then?"

Celeste grinned. "I have the perfect retaliation in mind —"

The painful blare of a car horn interrupted her words. Gabe realized he had been talking with Celeste as though the line of impatient drivers behind him didn't even exist.

He stared at her, for some reason wanting to say more, to keep her talking. Another horn blast disturbed his thoughts. "I'd better go."

"Right."

Gabe pulled his car forward and within two seconds, screeching alarms sounded. He'd forgotten to hand her his toll.

Celeste stepped out of the booth to retrieve the dollar bill, ignoring a loud wolf-whistle coming from the line of cars.

Gabe noticed the flush on her cheeks and also the heat in his own. But her smile

16

never wavered. She handled herself well in an embarrassing situation, he thought.

"Sorry," she said, "I forgot to hit the gate switch."

"No, it was my fault." He gazed into her smoky gray eyes which sparkled with amusement, as though she was enjoying herself.

"Thanks for the rose. It was a nice surprise."

"Happy birthday, Celeste."

"Enjoy the rest of the day," she replied softly.

Her lips were inches away from his as she bent to retrieve the toll. He could kiss her quite easily, he realized, shocked that he wanted to.

A soft breeze blew the sides of her hair against her cheek, causing Celeste to bring her hand to her face. He stared at her long, slender fingers. Each nail was painted a different color. On her it looked whimsical, not at all bizarre.

"Thanks a lot," she said.

Gabe watched in the rearview mirror as Celeste returned to the booth. Her hips swayed fetchingly and her skirt swirled around her legs. His gaze dropped to her feet, which were surprisingly bare.

As Celeste stepped into the booth, she paused and tilted her head toward him as though she knew he was still watching her. A dazzling smile caused her face to almost glow as she nodded at him, bringing the rose to her lips once again.

Gabe tore his gaze from her, forcing his thoughts back to the fact that he was now even more embarrassingly late for work.

Celeste bit her lower lip in frustration. Her shift relief was already fifteen minutes late, her patience was running thin, and she'd run out of cheerfulness. She was also having trouble keeping her attention on the job at hand.

All she could think about was getting back home, already behind schedule for her own busy day.

"Sorry I'm so late, Celeste. I'm Sandy, by the way. You were a doll to cover for me this morning and I really appreciate it. My little girl was so sick . . . but I got her into urgent care and over to my mom's as quick as I could. The doctor said the medicine should kick in quick."

Celeste jumped at the perky voice, startled by the jumble of words that interrupted her thoughts. She instantly forgave the young woman, canceling her negative thoughts, replacing them with sympathetic ones.

"It's all right, really. Don't worry about it. I hope it's nothing serious."

"Oh, no, just another earache. Has it been busy? I saw the sign when I drove up — did Kay do that?"

Celeste nodded as she continued to take tolls while the young woman stowed her purse and clocked in.

Sandy patted her hair and checked her teeth for lipstick in the always-have-a-smile-ready-for-the-customer mirror on the counter. "Kay's the best boss I've ever had. I never thought I'd keep as busy as she's kept me, working so many temp jobs and all."

Celeste struggled to concentrate on the woman's conversation. She didn't want to be rude, but she was more than ready to be on her way and wasn't in the mood to chit-chat.

"Thanks again. Hey, what's this?" The young woman picked up Gabe's rose from the counter and brought it to her face to breathe in its perfume. "Secret admirer?"

"Some guy in a Volvo," Celeste answered, her tone even and colorless.

"Some cute guy, I hope?" Sandy asked.

"Just a guy. Nothing special." Celeste felt a twinge of guilt at her misleading reply. Why did the encounter with the stranger seem special? She had no reason to even be thinking about him.

But she *was* thinking about him. That alone added to the strangeness. She'd noticed the floral box on the seat beside him, so she figured the whole event was just a spontaneous gesture on his part to join in on the birthday gag.

He was just another yuppie eager to play with the other rats in the rat race, Celeste reminded herself. Still, she allowed herself to dwell a moment on the memory of the expression in his chocolate brown eyes. Eyes that seemed honest, even a little naive. Hmmm . . .

"Celeste?"

"What?" She shook away the memory of the stranger.

"I'm ready when you are." Sandy touched her arm and they smoothly changed places in the tollbooth.

Celeste took the rose from Sandy, then clocked out, slipped her feet into her sandals, and grabbed her purse. She waited until the approaching car came to a stop at the booth and then ran to her pale blue Volkswagen van.

Normally when she filled in at the tollbooth to help out her friend Kay, the job was pleasant, mindless work. Almost therapeutic compared to anything she'd ever done in her life. Today had been a dramatic exception, reminding her how much she loved having her own business, being her own boss.

As soon as she turned her van around and aimed for home, her brain kicked back into work mode. She lowered the volume of the soothing sounds of piano music that filled the interior of her van. Mentally she began to make a list. Place her supply order before noon. Do a new price comparison of floral boxes. Proof the Yellow Pages ad. Enter last week's expenses into the computer.

And find out exactly what was delaying her latest potential account from making a decision. Didn't they realize she had a business to run?

Celeste rubbed her forehead, now wrinkled with the tension of her thoughts. At a stoplight, she breathed deeply, commanding herself to ease the pressure that was building.

Remember, you left the corporate world so you wouldn't have to feel this kind of stress, she reminded herself. Celeste ejected the tape from her cassette player and the radio announcer's voice filled the van.

"This is Charlie Chattham signing off on my last Monday morning of my last week at wonderful KGLD, your station of golden oldies and magical memories —"

"And don't forget endless delays, guys."

Celeste snapped off the radio as she pulled into her driveway, anxious to get her real day underway.

She grabbed her things and almost ran up the walk to the beach cottage she had called home for almost a year now. As she closed the door behind her, she glanced at the blinking light on her answering machine. "Better be good news."

She immediately hit the play button and waited for the message to rewind.

"Celeste, this is Brent, Sales Manager at KGLD, and we still haven't made a final decision about using Celestial Cookies for the Valentine campaign. Our new morning DJ, Gabe Freeman, has some reservations and we needed to ask you —"

The machine screeched, interrupting the message in midstream.

"Ask me what?" she said, shaking her head and mentally adding "buy new answering machine" to her to-do list.

Celeste grabbed her keys and headed back out the door. It was time for the radio station to make a decision and it looked like she'd need to go there in person to make it happen.

She had her own deadlines. If she was going to service their upcoming Valentine's Day promotion, she needed to buy triple her normal supplies, and the supply order needed to be called in within the next few hours.

Enough was enough. They either make a decision today or she would withdraw her proposal, she decided.

Just as the words formed in her head, another thought followed. *But you really need this account,* the voice in her head whispered.

It was true. Her gourmet cookie business was steadily growing but she had a new oven to pay for and bills that needed more attention than she'd been able to give them since she'd plunged headfirst into self-employment.

The radio account was more important than she wanted to admit. Resigning herself to the fact that she might need to do some major schmoozing, Celeste did an abrupt about-face and went back into the house.

Inside, she grabbed a decorative tin of chocolate chip cookies. She would use them to tantalize and tempt the stubborn morning DJ that was causing all her head-aches.

A smile replaced her frown. Gabe Free-man wouldn't even know what hit him. She was determined to leave the radio station with a signed contract, no matter what it took.

Two

Celeste pulled into the KGLD parking lot, choosing a visitor spot perpendicular to the busy main street. She figured she might as well take advantage of the drive-by traffic.

Just a week ago she'd had her van custom painted to help advertise Celestial Cookies. It now featured air-brushed chocolate chip cookies — complete with angel wings — flying through blue sky and puffy white clouds. After much contemplation, she'd decided to use her business card design to create a mobile billboard of her classic VW van.

Her company name and phone number were prominently featured in metallic blue script. The effect was eye-catching and she'd already received a dozen calls from people who'd seen the van around town.

It had been an expensive investment, but Celeste was convinced it would soon pay for itself in new cookie customers.

Celeste stood in front of the main desk

in the lobby and waited until the receptionist finished her call, then opened the tin, allowing the concentrated aroma of freshly baked cookies to escape.

"Hi, how can I help you?" The young woman barely looked at Celeste, the words being spoken almost mechanically.

"Just baked these this morning." Celeste watched as the receptionist closed her eyes, deeply breathing the scent rising from the tin like an invisible heavenly cloud.

"Glad I skipped breakfast this morning. One couldn't hurt, could it?"

Celeste glanced down at the nameplate on the desk. "Shelly, is there any way you can get me in to see Gabe Freeman?"

Shelly delicately bit into the cookie and closed her eyes again. "These are *wonderful* . . . homemade's my weakness."

"Glad you like it. Why don't you take another one for later," Celeste urged. More than once she'd noticed the unusually dramatic effect her cookies seemed to have on people.

Shelly grinned her acceptance and took another cookie from the tin. "One for the road —"

"And about Mr. Freeman?" Celeste asked again, hoping she had adequately sweetened the receptionist into compliance.

"Pardon me?" Shelly's voice had a dreamy quality as she finished eating the cookie. "It just melts in your mouth."

"I'm Celeste Parker — of Celestial Cookies — and I *really* need to talk to Mr. Freeman about the Valentine's Day promotion."

"Well, I'm not supposed to, but I could put you in Gabe's office — and find him and send him there, if you like," Shelly said.

"That would be perfect. I promise not to take up much of his time," Celeste assured her. *One down and one to go,* she thought. She knew well the power of making friends with the receptionist and Shelly was now behaving like her newest best friend.

"Follow me." Shelly pressed a buzzer under her desk and indicated for Celeste to come with her through a secured door.

"Oh, Gabe, they're beautiful," Jillian murmured as she unfolded the white tissue and carefully scooped the red roses from the box that sat in the middle of the glass-topped table she used as her desk.

Gabe watched as she meticulously arranged the stems in a crystal vase that was already filled with water. As usual, Jillian was well prepared for the expected arrival of the roses.

A week ago, she'd made it quite clear to him that it was appropriate to mark the six-month date before their wedding with the groom-to-be presenting a gift of flowers to the bride-to-be. Gabe sighed. It had already been a rather tedious six months of learning every form imaginable of pre-wedding etiquette — and following every rule and protocol directed by the expensive wedding planner Jillian had hired.

Much to his dismay, the wedding preparations had become something he had to deal with on an almost daily basis.

Part of him questioned what all the fuss and bother was about, but he tried to empathize with Jillian. Big, elaborate weddings were important to most women, he knew. And by the looks of it, theirs was going to be a doozie.

"What florist did you use?" Jillian's voice held an irritated edge, somewhere between disappointed and annoyed.

"What?" Gabe tried to shake loose the lingering mood of distraction he still felt. While he stared at his fiancée, he couldn't quite get the picture of tollbooth Celeste out of his mind. As he'd neared the station, he had even missed his turn, having to double back to make his way into the entrance of the parking lot.

"There are only eleven roses here, Gabe. Whoever you used, don't use them again." Her tone was patronizing as she further inspected each bloom.

Gabe felt heat flush his cheeks. What was he supposed to say? One thing he was very sure of — Jillian would not understand, let alone approve of, his impulse to give one of *her* roses to a beautiful stranger at a tollbooth.

"Here you two are." Jillian's father walked into the office, his loud baritone interrupting the conversation.

"Hi, Dad. Aren't these gorgeous? Only six more months until the big day." Jillian planted a quick kiss on her father's cheek, turning her back to Gabe.

"Say, that's right — doesn't time fly? Seems like only yesterday when I threw you two together, doesn't it?" Her father wrapped his arm around Jillian's slender waist. "I'm awfully glad you both came to your senses and decided to take the big plunge."

Gabe fought from grimacing at his future father-in-law's remarks. Marrying the boss's daughter had once been the farthest thing from his mind, but later it seemed like the rational thing to do. Even Jillian had agreed with the logic behind it.

They were fairly compatible, had similar tastes and styles, and both were too busy to spend much time within the singles scene. She seemed fond of him, and he didn't expect the passion and fireworks. Romance, to him, was somewhat unreal, not something to truly strive for.

Theirs was a modern, sensible agreement — a practical merger, actually.

The marriage would reinforce both their careers, and the idea definitely pleased Jillian's father immensely. And Gabe had quickly learned how important that was to her.

Jillian was her father's daughter, anxious to follow in his footsteps, and always anxious to please him. In the end, it had even been she who had first suggested the idea of marriage. She'd presented the proposal to him in precise detail, listing the pros and cons as though they were in a business meeting.

An unexpected shudder ran up Gabe's spine. Until today, it had seemed like a completely acceptable notion.

The phone buzzed on Jillian's desk, signaling an internal call. Jillian punched the speaker button. "Yes?"

"Actually, I'm looking for Gabe, Jillian."

Gabe leaned toward the phone. "I'm

here, Brent. What's up?"

"Sales meeting. Conference room. Fifteen minutes."

So, the morning meeting had not started without him. In fact, Gabe's late arrival had not even been mentioned, though he had noticed Jillian's father glancing at his watch when he'd greeted him earlier.

Jillian punched the speaker button to end the call, turning again toward her father.

"Valentine's Day?"

Her father nodded, raising an eyebrow and giving a slight nod toward Gabe. "He's not so sure about using Celestial Cookies to tie in with the listener call-in promotion."

Gabe felt Jillian's glare before he looked up to check her expression.

Again, the phone buzzed.

Jillian hit the speaker button and answered through tight lips, "Yes, what is it?"

This time, it was the sugary sweet voice of the receptionist. "Is Gabe there?"

"I'm on my way back to my office, Shelly. I'll take the call there, thanks." Gabe seized the opportunity to end the uncomfortable discussion in Jillian's office. With any luck, it would be a short call and at least he'd have a little time to get his thoughts collected before the sales meeting.

"See you in a few," he called over his shoulder at Jillian and her father who were already deep in discussion over the listener demographic reports on her desk.

Gabe made quick time in reaching his office down the hall. He flung open the door and walked to his desk, immediately realizing his phone was not flashing a call-on-hold light.

Without looking up, he pressed the front desk intercom button. "Did we lose the call, Shelly?"

"Actually, it's not a call, Gabe. There's someone in your office to see you."

Gabe finally looked up. He disconnected the intercom as he stared at the woman standing opposite him. Celeste? Tollbooth Celeste? A slight dizziness accompanied his surprise as his thoughts raced to make sense of the situation.

He continued to stare at her, simultaneously confused at both her appearance and his own unexpected feeling of delight. He'd never anticipated seeing this particular birthday girl again in his lifetime, let alone find her standing in his office within an hour of meeting her.

Celeste extended her hand toward him.

He gazed at it. Multi-colored nails. Silver bangles. He looked up, dumbfounded . . . and speechless.

Celeste cleared her throat. "Well, this *is* a surprise. I'm Celeste Parker and you must be Gabe Freeman." Her hand still suspended in the air between them, Celeste fought to control her voice, hoping it sounded more confident than she felt.

Gabe finally reached out his own hand, firmly grasping hers as he shook his head in dismay.

"What can I do for you, Celeste?"

"Well, actually, I brought something for you." Celeste withdrew her hand, then placed the tin on the desk between them and lifted the lid. She looked up to gauge his reaction, but his gaze was still frozen on her face.

"I'm the owner of Celestial Cookies — the Valentine's Day promotion . . . ?" Celeste struggled to make her voice sound self-assured. Inside, she felt totally out of control, her stomach squishy with the nervousness she felt.

She'd been prepared to march into the radio station and fast-talk her way through a stubborn jerk's resistance to using her product for the advertising campaign. Instead, she found herself talking with the handsome stranger who had spontaneously given her a perfect rose just because it was her birthday.

Gabe finally blinked and looked down at his desk, down at the cherub-decorated tin sitting there, filled with cookies.

"Celestial Cookies?" he asked.

"Yup, that's me. Won't you try one before you make a decision about the promotion? People really love my cookies . . ." Her voice faded to a whisper. Now that was certainly not the most intelligent thing I've ever said, she thought.

She was thankful that Gabe didn't even seem to be listening to her. He slowly reached toward the tin and selected a cookie. She watched as he bit, chewed, and swallowed.

His eyes revealed his evident pleasure, and Celeste waited for his positive comments.

"They're pretty good," he began, "but I'm still not convinced we should do the promotion."

Celeste narrowed her eyes as she scrutinized Gabe's face. His brown eyes now masked his pleasure — merely proclaiming polite interest. "Why?" she asked.

"Well, I just think we need to explore all of our options."

"Of course you should. That's why I decided to see you to give my proposal a . . . a personal touch."

She continued, finally beginning to feel more confident, falling into the comfortable role of salesperson. "Is there any reason why you think using my cookie bouquets is a bad idea?"

Gabe stared at her mouth, watching her full lips speak words that he barely heard. What was it about her that attracted him? Maybe because she was so . . . different, he guessed. Up close, her complexion was flawless. She wore little makeup, not much more than lip and cheek color.

He stared at her hair, still a little wild-looking even out of the breeze. She was attractive in a very unconventional way. *Eye candy,* his brain whispered. Gabe blinked in confusion, suffering a little from a pleasurable sensory overload.

Celeste stood before him as though she had all the time in the world. And time itself seemed to have stopped for a moment. As he leaned forward, her gaze never faltered.

He stared in her eyes, eyes the color of clouds readying for a gentle rain, and watched as the corners of her lips turned up into a soft smile.

Gabe chewed another bite of cookie, praying his mental faculties would return so he could figure out what to say to her. The cookie's flavor exploded in his mouth. He'd never tasted anything so . . . what was it? Buttery? There was some different, extra flavor. And they contained more vanilla, he decided. If it was a taste test there would be no decision, he knew. Celeste's cookies would win hands down.

Celeste reached her hand toward him, her silver bangles sliding toward her elbow. Then she reached one purple-tipped finger toward him, gently brushing a crumb from his chin.

He wanted like crazy to kiss her.

"You ready for the sales meeting?"

Gabe tore his gaze from Celeste and looked over her shoulder to see Jillian standing in the doorway.

"Jillian . . ."

"Brent's waiting. Will you be long?"

Jillian's voice sounded quite neutral, betraying no reaction to either Celeste or the fact that he was leaning toward her, passionate kisses still on his mind.

"Jillian Caufield, this is Celeste —"

"— Parker." Celeste finished the introduction, turning toward Jillian. "Of Celestial Cookies." She was surprised to find she could control her voice, hoping like hell her words sounded more composed than she felt.

Jillian stepped into the room and offered her hand to Celeste. "I've just looked at our demographics and I'd say your product is perfect for the campaign, right, Gabe?"

"We haven't made our final decision yet."

Jillian shot him a dagger glare. "As I was saying, the demographics and all the other market research indicates the cookies are a good choice."

Gabe clenched his jaws. Though this was definitely not the hill he wished to die on, he was disappointed in Jillian's outright support of the campaign, regardless of his opinion. And it was supposed to be *his* decision, as the new morning DJ. The Valentine's Day promotion would also launch his debut morning appearance on KGLD.

"Right, Gabe?" Jillian continued her glare, waiting for his response.

Celeste reached for the tin of cookies. "Would you like one? They're fresh-baked this morning and I —"

"No thanks. Wouldn't be worth the fat content and calories." Jillian raised her chin and gave Celeste a chilly look.

Celeste held her gaze. "Right. Well, perhaps I should call later and —"

Gabe interrupted her. "That won't be necessary. Looks like Celestial Cookies is the confirmed choice. Congratulations."

Celeste nodded her head in a small gesture of thanks. "Great, so what's next?"

"Actually," Jillian began. "Why don't you join us? The sales crew is anxious to get things started."

Now this should be interesting, Celeste thought. At least the tension in the room had eased enough to be tolerable. She hoped the sales meeting wouldn't heat things up again.

Gabe's face seemed slightly pale as he smiled at them both. "Let's go," he said, grabbing a portfolio and pen.

Gabe led the way down the hallway in long purposeful strides. He was anxious to get through the meeting and more than anxious to have Celeste on her way. Distractions he didn't need, he reminded himself. With any luck, the marketing meeting would go without a hitch and things would get back to normal.

Back to *feeling* normal. He was baffled by both his powerful attraction to Celeste and his more than minor irritation with Jillian.

"Oh, by the way, Celeste, how do you

feel about helping out with the voiceovers for the commercials?" Jillian asked.

"Sure," Celeste answered.

Gabe was too startled by the question to offer any objection. Okay, how long could it take to record a few commercials, he thought. Then she would be gone.

Jillian continued. "As part of the campaign to launch Gabe as the new morning DJ, he'll be going out with you each afternoon to deliver the cookie bouquets to each winning call-in entry."

Three

"Everyone," Jillian began, her voice sounding triumphant from her recent victory over Gabe's indecision, "this is Celeste Parker of Celestial Cookies."

Gabe sat to the left of Jillian's father, watching Celeste make her rounds, shaking hands with the ad execs already seated around the conference table.

Completing her circuit, she shook hands with Jillian's father.

"I'm George Caufield. Welcome to the snakepit, Celeste." Jillian's father pulled out the remaining empty chair, putting her directly opposite Gabe.

"Glad to be here, Mr. Caufield." She flashed Gabe a smile as she settled into her place at the table.

They would eat her alive, he thought. More than once he'd witnessed the sales crew's raucous, cutthroat behavior.

"Let's get started," Celeste began, "now, who can give me a bullet point description of the campaign and both the statistical goals and the revenue goals you have targeted?"

Gabe could almost hear jaws drop as the sales crew stared at Celeste in shock.

Jillian broke the silence, responding with a jumble of demographics and sales statistics. She was in her glory when it came to revenue analysis and the effect of listener promotions.

"Listeners will call in to our Valentine Loveline from seven to eleven in the morning," Jillian continued, "and leave a message as to why their Valentine deserves a cookie bouquet."

Gabe watched as Jillian glanced coolly toward Celeste. He also noticed that she caught everyone's gaze but his. Probably still perturbed with his resistance to the campaign, he reasoned.

"Gabe will play some of the messages during his a.m. air time during the two weeks before the holiday."

"How many winners per day?" Celeste asked.

"At the end of the morning show," Jillian resumed, ignoring her question, "you and Gabe will select a winner from each hour and deliver a cookie bouquet to each winner that afternoon."

"So, four each day," Celeste interjected.

Her tone was even, deliberately polite.

"Yes, as I was saying . . ."

"So, four each day for two weeks — are the weeks calendar weeks or work weeks?" Celeste asked.

Gabe cringed. Jillian detested interruptions. When she had something to present, he'd learned to let her have her say and wait for her consent before bothering to reply. Today, her routine seemed more annoying than usual to him.

And it was quite obvious that Celeste was not playing along. Gabe smiled and nodded. He had a feeling that Celeste might look naive, but she knew how to swim with the sharks.

"Work weeks." Jillian glared at Celeste.

Jillian's father drummed his fingers on the table and cleared his throat. "Celeste, why don't you and Gabe join Brent in the sound booth and get started on the commercial spots. I'd like to announce the promotion on the air tomorrow."

In immediate response, chairs scooted away from the table and the room emptied within minutes. Gabe shook his head as he silently followed Celeste and Brent to the sound booth.

Celeste sat in her van, her fingers rubbing at the tension that had accumulated in her neck muscles. After a few laughter-filled starts, the voiceovers had gone exceptionally well.

Even so, she was very glad the morning was finally over.

And the worst part had been sharing the microphone with Gabe, she thought. Every time they'd leaned intimately close together to record their dialogue, the butterflies in her stomach felt like they were going to escape by way of her throat.

Why did he affect her so intensely? She shuddered. And it had been difficult being in such familiar territory; the tension of the sales meeting, surrounded by over-eager ad execs, each ready to sacrifice the rest to get ahead.

She had to admit she'd enjoyed the fact the crew hadn't expected her to be aware of what listener campaigns meant to business. She'd smugly kept to herself the fact that radio campaigns had been her specialty when she was one of them.

Celeste sighed and glanced in the mirror. For a split second, she imagined her old self. Dark, designer suit. Expensive, understated jewelry. Italian pumps. Kick-ass attitude. And, she realized, Jillian could have been her twin. Except for Jillian's impossibly light blond hair and turquoise eyes, the similarities were definitely there, she admitted.

"Never again," she muttered, turning the key in the ignition, pumping the gas pedal to coax the van's engine to life.

And Gabe Freeman was one of them, she reminded herself, though she had to concede he'd been quite easygoing during the recording session. And the end result was good — their spots had a chemistry that she knew would entice listeners to call in.

It would be a good promotion. She could feel it in her very experienced bones.

"Thanks a lot, Celeste. That's the last time I'm ever going to make your birthday memorable," Kay said.

Celeste grinned, shouldering the phone. She put the finishing touches of navy blue nail polish on Kay's oldest daughter. She'd already sent the younger two home to show their mom their makeovers, causing Kay's immediate phone call.

"I think they look adorable," Celeste said, "and besides, they think they look adorable. You know how you're always so concerned about their self-esteem."

She knew Kay would have no argument.

"Kay, don't stay mad and come on over," Celeste said. "Maybe you and the girls could help me catch up. I'm about four hours behind schedule today."

"I'm hanging up now," Kay replied.

Celeste hung up the receiver and re-placed the lid on the bottle of polish. "Blow on your nails like this, Angela." She showed the eight-year-old how to curl her fingers and move them in front of her pursed lips. "That's it."

Kay walked into Celeste's kitchen, her five-year-old twins close on her heels. Annie carefully balanced a plateful of chocolate cupcakes and Anessa carried brightly colored paper plates and napkins.

"Happy birthday, Celeste," the twins shouted.

Celeste sighed. Another delay, she thought. Although part of her was secretly glad not to have to face her fortieth birth-day alone and with nothing to do, it was getting a little ridiculous.

"Thanks, guys. Did you bake those cup-cakes?" she asked.

The twins nodded until their pigtails bounced.

Angela paused in her nail blowing just long enough to add, "And I frosted them and put on the sprinkles."

"And I licked the bowl," Kay added, causing all three of her daughters to collapse into giggles.

In Celeste's mind, Kay was the epitome of the successful single mom, and she cherished her friendship. She also loved the interaction with Kay's daughters, who daily caused her heart to swell. It had been a surprise to her. She'd never thought of herself as having much maternal instinct.

The first time she had agreed to Kay's request to baby-sit on short notice, Celeste had discovered how much fun the three girls were. Since then, she'd become almost a second mom.

Kay pointed to the single rose in the delicately etched crystal vase on the kitchen counter. "So, what's this all about?" Her voice was shaded with exaggerated interest.

"Long story." Celeste reached up to smooth her wavy hair away from her face. Her finger caught a lock of hair, twirling a long curl until it was wrapped completely around her finger.

"I've got the time. Unless you have other plans —"

Celeste cut her words off with a glare. "My plans are to try to catch up from losing half my day helping you out at the tollbooths."

Kay ignored her remark and reached over to put Annie's napkin in her lap. "Try not to drop crumbs, sweetie. Goodness' sakes, my girls make yummy cupcakes — don't they, Celeste?"

"Sure do," she agreed. "Guess they take after me." Celeste lifted her chin in exaggerated pride. In the year she'd lived next door to Kay, she'd learned a great deal. In the first month she'd seen the end of Kay's abusive marriage, shortly after Kay's discovery that her husband had once again blown the grocery and rent money on drugs. Then Celeste had helped Kay research and successfully complete do-it-yourself divorce proceedings.

She'd also witnessed how strong Kay was and how, amazingly, she still believed in marriage. She was even dating. She'd carefully talked with her girls about it, though, and introduced her beau to them on neutral ground to test their reaction.

Luckily, they'd fallen head over heels for Jack. He was a good man. Hard working. Blue collar all the way. And he was patient. He knew both Kay and the girls needed time to learn how to trust again.

"So?" Kay softly punched Celeste's arm to regain her attention.

"Okay, short version. This guy in a Volvo

came through the tollbooth and handed the rose to me instead of the toll," she said. She purposely left out details about how he'd made her feel — how she still felt. Her cheeks burned just remembering his adorable, embarrassed expression when the toll alarms had sounded.

"Then I came home and there's half a message from the radio station, so I decide to go over there and talk some sense into them and —"

"Does Volvo Man works at the radio station?" Kay asked.

"His name is Gabe Freeman, and he's the one who has been holding up the decision to use Celestial Cookies, in fact."

"What does he look like?"

Celeste threw her a warning glare. "I'm pretty sure he's involved."

"How do you know? And so what if he is?" Kay's eyes widened in feigned innocence.

Celeste's thoughts froze. She was fairly certain the tension between Jillian and Gabe stemmed from an office romance of some kind. It was classic. When Jillian had declared her support for using Celestial Cookies for the promotion, she'd sensed Gabe's calculated decision to abandon his opposition.

And she would gamble big bucks that Gabe's decision was at least partially based on how much it would affect his and Jillian's relationship, not to mention the fact that his fiancée was the boss' daughter.

"Details," Kay coaxed.

"Okay." Celeste took a deep breath. Kay was her friend, she reminded herself. Someone to really talk to, confide in. "He's a suit just like —" Her words ended abruptly.

"Like Wade," Kay finished, reaching out her hand to touch her friend's arm.

She helped Celeste in every way she could after Wade's sudden death at forty-two of a stress-induced heart attack, and understood that her friend's marriage to him hadn't been all that happy.

Celeste inhaled sharply, lifting her chin a little before she continued. "Very ambitious," she said. "Nice clothes, expensive taste, corporate all the way."

Kay stared at her, her eyes squinting. "But cute, I'd say, by your deliberate lack of physical description."

Celeste paused. "He's drop-dead gorgeous, actually. Very *GQ*. Fit. Short brown hair and big, brown eyes. Eyelashes to die for. And funny. And good at what he does, I think."

"Ah, that's better, now we're getting somewhere." Kay grinned. "Girls, I bet your show's on. Why don't you go in Celeste's TV room for a little while?"

The three girls bounded out of their chairs to take advantage of the special treat of television in the afternoon.

"So, are you going to see him again?"

Celeste rolled her eyes. "Every day for the next two weeks. We have to pick the winning call-in Valentine message each hour and then deliver four cookie bouquets each afternoon."

"Interesting opportunity to get to know each other," Kay commented. "So, what exactly are you afraid of?"

"Honestly?" Celeste bit her lower lip. "Spending that much time with him. I'm . . . attracted to him."

"So, what's wrong with that?"

"I don't want to be, for one thing. He's not what I would be looking for even if I was looking."

"Oh, come on," Kay's voice dropped in volume. "You can't possibly think it's rational to cross every eager executive off your list just because of what happened to Wade."

Celeste balled up her napkin. "On the way home from the meeting, I just kept having flashbacks, you know? Intense sales meetings. Everybody twitching from too much caffeine and ambition. I feel so lucky to be out of that environment."

"I know. And you've done wonders with your business. And I've watched you grow with it," Kay said.

Celeste realized she had changed. She didn't have to assimilate the tension of Gabe's world. She didn't even have to get involved in Gabe's world. He was just an account.

"You've learned how to balance," Kay said, "and you need to trust yourself. Just go with the flow."

Celeste nodded. She had to confess she at least half believed Kay's remarks. But could she spend hours every day for two weeks with a man who made her feel the way Gabe made her feel — a man she wanted to run from *and* run to?

Four

"The love of my life is the hardest working handyman in San Diego — and he's been the best husband to me and father to our five kids. He makes me feel like it's Valentine's Day every day."

Celeste turned up the volume on the radio in her van. Her stomach betrayed her nervousness with its rumblings and queasiness. A combination of dread and elation filled her as she drove to KGLD to pick the first day's winners of cookie bouquets.

The promotion had launched without a hitch and the Loveline phones had been jammed from the campaign's kickoff.

The sound of Gabe's deep, velvety voice reverberated in the cab of the van as he identified the artists and song titles of the previous set of love songs. Slowing to a stop at a red light, Celeste stared at the radio, listening intently.

"Well, listeners, we have another Valentine nominee — another handyman with 'good hands.' I hope the rest of you can be a little more creative than that. Call in your Valentine message to KGLD's Love-line for your chance to win a Celestial Cookie bouquet. Now, let's get back to our next nonstop music set . . ."

Celeste shook her head, her jaw clenched. Obviously, Gabe wasn't taking the promotion very seriously. His voice dripped with sarcasm and disinterest.

She stared at the traffic light, willing it to be green.

Her own success was riding on the campaign, too, she thought. Mr. Caufield had made it clear that her part in the promotion was equally important — and her reputation in the business community would be affected, she knew. By Gabe's lack of enthusiasm, it appeared he was more determined to create failure than triumph.

Celeste punched the gas pedal and left more than a little rubber behind in the intersection. What was he thinking? Maybe she was wrong about him. Maybe he didn't have enough heart or brains to pull it off — to make the promotion appeal to his listeners regardless of how he personally felt about it.

She pulled into the radio station's lot, parked her van, and marched into the lobby. The receptionist grinned and waved, then buzzed open the door behind her desk.

Celeste walked quickly down the hallway, just glimpsing the back of Gabe's head as he ducked into his office. She increased her pace, walking through a cloud of his cologne — a musky, lavender scent that unexpectedly distracted her from her fury.

Celeste stopped dead in her tracks. Forcing herself to take a few deep, measured breaths, she closed her eyes. Old habits die hard, she thought, not really surprised to find herself instinctively fuming and ready to attack Gabe for his lack of support.

Just as quickly, she realized she should step back and try to discover why he was still so resistant to the campaign.

Her control reinstated, Celeste stepped into the doorway and knocked on the door frame to get Gabe's attention.

Gabe was sitting at his desk sorting a pile of papers when he looked up to see Celeste. She looked less like a gypsy but she still unnerved him with her casual, noncorporate attire. She wore a long, gauzy dress in a maroon Indian print that hugged her curves; cinched at the waist with a scarf woven with golden, sparkling threads. At the ends of the scarf, gold-toned bells hung, tinkling as she walked into the room.

Celeste stopped in front of his desk and stood, arms folded against her chest. "Hi, partner. Ready to pick today's winners and get this show on the road?" she asked.

Suddenly, Gabe felt he needed time to compose himself. "Be with you in one minute. Let me just finish up here and I'll meet you in the sound booth." Even to himself, his voice sounded overly flat, overly controlled.

"Right." Celeste pivoted and walked out of his office. He stared at her, his attention focused on the swirl of her skirt and the swing of her dark curls against her impossibly pale, delicate neck. This was business, he reminded himself. She's just an account, just here to do her job.

Pulling a handkerchief out of his pocket, he dabbed at the perspiration on his forehead, irritated at her effect on him.

As he stood in the doorway of the sound booth, Gabe watched as Celeste concentrated on Brent's instructions on the operation of the tape deck. She cocked her head as she listened to him, occasionally nodding and glancing at the dials and knobs on the console, rewarding Brent with a dazzling smile when he concluded.

Gabe sighed, his lips tightening into a grimace. He knew he needed to just relax and get through the next couple of weeks. With any luck, life would feel normal again soon.

"Are we ready?" he said, walking into the room.

"She's a natural, Gabe," Brent said. "I've got each hour's messages cued up, ready for you to listen to. I'll bring you the list of names and addresses as soon as Shelly types them up."

Celeste remained silent, her gaze meeting his. Gabe loosened his tie and looked away. "Okay, let's make this quick. I've already got a ton of reports to look over and mail to open."

"Call me if you need anything," Brent said, directing his comment to Celeste as he left the room.

"Thanks, I think we'll be fine. See you later, Brent." Celeste returned her attention to the sound board and started the tape. "Have a seat and we'll get started."

Gabe nodded and sat in the chair next to her. He breathed in the unexpected aroma of vanilla as she leaned over the board, adjusting the volume as the first Loveline message began to play.

"My daddy's my Valentine. He loves me more than anything in the whole wide world and he tells me that every night."

As the message ended, Gabe reached to press the pause button, his arm brushing against Celeste's shoulder. He caught his breath as she turned toward him, her cheek within inches of his.

Gabe cleared his throat. "Maybe we ought to discuss our strategy for picking the winners."

"Well, based on your on-air commentary, I figured you didn't have much concern about actually choosing the best message, as long as it was clever."

Gabe stared at her face and watched as her stormy gray eyes narrowed when she met his gaze. "What do you mean?" he asked.

"I mean, it doesn't seem to me that you are sold on this campaign and I figured you wouldn't even want to be a part of choosing the winners. Am I wrong?"

Gabe sat back in his chair and mentally gave her high marks for intuition. Besides, what did he know about true love and Valentine wishes?

"Look," Celeste began, "I don't mean to be rude. This campaign affects my business success too, and I would rather deal with someone who at least appears to support the promotion. Your listeners are going to pick up on your sarcasm pretty quickly and it will influence the tone of this campaign."

Gabe looked away. She was right. He rubbed his temples to soothe the tension headache that had developed during the morning. It was a sure sign he was uncomfortable with what he was doing.

"Let's just go through this first batch and we'll give each message a score on a scale of one to ten. When we're done, we'll compare notes and see where we are. Maybe we'll luck out and narrow the messages down and be able to settle on a winner."

Gabe nodded. "And we could always flip a coin," he added. He glanced toward her and saw her face brighten a little, rewarding his glib comment with a heart-stopping smile.

"Good." Celeste pressed the pause button again, returning her attention to the sound of the next message.

They had settled fairly smoothly on four winners: an unemployed ship builder, the fiancé of an exotic dancer, a stay-at-home dad, and the wife of an insurance salesman.

Shelly had brought them deli sandwiches while they worked and, eventually, the names and addresses of the callers. Celeste had looked at the list, matched up the winners and then went out to her van to put together a delivery route.

Gabe watched Celeste leave, then walked to his office. Celeste expected him to meet her in the parking lot in ten minutes leaving him with just enough time to check his voicemail before embarking on their first cookie delivery. He picked up the phone, accessed his voicemail and listened to the first message.

"Gabe, it's Jillian. Don't be late for our appointment with the caterer this afternoon at four-thirty. My office."

Gabe groaned and erased the message. As if he cared what appetizers were served before the rehearsal dinner, he thought, shuddering at the details that still remained in the wedding planning. He wished Jillian would just proceed with the decision-making without him since his opinion rarely mattered anyway.

It was going to be a long day — even longer with the added appointment with the caterer.

Gabe gazed out the office window. The morning fog had lifted, making the weather unseasonably warm and sunny. Impulsively, he removed his jacket and tie. After all, he thought, he had no one to impress and schlepping cookie bouquets in a coat and tie in eighty-degree weather was quickly becoming unappealing.

Celeste drummed her fingers on the steering wheel as she stared in the rearview mirror, watching for Gabe. Finally the office door opened and Gabe stepped out into the sunshine. He cupped his hands over his eyes as he scanned the lot. His coat and tie were gone, she noticed, and he'd rolled up the sleeves of his light olive-colored, denim shirt. He seemed much more relaxed — almost casual. It suited him, she thought.

Gabe's hand rose to wave at her when he spotted the van. Celeste inhaled sharply, wiping her damp palms on her skirt. Why did she feel nervous? It was ridiculous. She'd given presentations to rooms filled with top executives and corporate CEOs and here she was, sitting there, her stomach in knots at the thought of spending the next few hours with a . . . a disc jockey.

"Did you design the graphics?" Gabe asked as he opened the door and climbed into the van.

Celeste nodded. "My neighbor came up with the name. Her daughter came up with the flying cookies. Too cute?" she asked.

Gabe shrugged. "It's an attention grabber — that's the whole idea, I guess."

Celeste raised a skeptical eyebrow. She'd have bet money he would have criticized the chocolate chip cookies with angel wings.

"God, it smells so good in here — how do you stand it?" Gabe audibly inhaled as he looked over his shoulder at the stacks of floral boxes, tins, and baskets of cookies.

"I try not to breathe too deeply." Celeste laughed. "I think I've put on fifteen pounds just from the aroma."

"Why do all women think they're over-weight?"

Celeste backed carefully out of the parking space. "Hmm, take your jacket and tie off and you turn into Mr. Curious, don't you?"

"Sorry. It's just that I've never quite fig-ured out why women assume all guys really think thin is the way all women should be."

Celeste paused at the end of the driveway and turned toward him. "Who are you and what have you done with Gabe Freeman?"

Gabe realized he felt very, very calm.

61

Must be a reaction to the smell of these damn cookies, he thought. Strangely, he felt like talking — really talking — to Celeste. He grinned, reaching for a plastic bag of broken cookies that was on the floor between them. "I intend to blame the cookies," he said.

They rode in comfortable silence as Celeste headed toward the freeway to take them to their first delivery destination.

Gabe munched on cookies, gazing at the scenery, appearing very contented. "It's a treat to be a passenger," he said. "Why is it that women never drive — when they're with a guy, I mean?"

"Well, I'd say it's usually because the guy criticizes their driving or insists on taking a route she didn't plan to take."

"You look like you like to drive."

Celeste thought for a moment. Her late husband had been an impossible passenger. It had always been easier to just let him drive while she sat quietly filing her nails to distract herself from commenting on his constant tailgating and weaving.

And besides, she loved the old delivery van she'd chosen, quickly growing used to sitting tall, above the majority of sedans and coupes on the road. She'd been surprised how easily she'd given up her baby

Benz for the practical vehicle.

"I do like to drive . . . now." She reached toward Gabe, taking a large cookie piece from the bag. "And when I tell you to take those away from me," she said, arching an eyebrow, "I expect you to comply with my request."

"Yeah, right." He chuckled easily. "I thought people got sick of whatever it was they had to dish up. My sister worked in an ice cream parlor in high school — didn't touch the stuff for years."

"I wish it was true," Celeste said. She had put on fifteen pounds since she'd started the business, but not from breathing cookie aroma. She'd realized that she no longer obsessed about the size of her waist and was growing comfortable with what she thought of as her new voluptuousness.

"And you," Gabe began, "do you think you're overweight?"

Celeste felt heat flush her cheeks. "Are you going to be this personal for the rest of the day?"

"Does it bother you?"

Celeste thought a bit before she answered. She felt confused, but she didn't really feel bothered by his questions. What was peculiar was feeling the urge to answer him honestly.

63

"There's our exit," Gabe pointed at a freeway marker.

"Thanks." She probably would have missed the turn, her thoughts were so entangled. "Okay. We can talk," she began, "but let's set some ground rules."

"Fair enough."

"If it gets too personal or controversial, we each have the right to end the conversation."

"Agreed."

"Okay, in answer to your question," she said, "I used to be more concerned about my weight, but I've consciously decided to not worry about it. I seem actually healthier with a few extra pounds and I no longer admire the emaciated models you see everywhere. I'm basically happy with how I look."

"See what I mean? You do think you're overweight . . . and you're not. That's what I'm saying. All men don't necessarily find thin women attractive. And I won't even mention how utterly annoying it is to go out to eat and she orders a dinner salad and a plain baked potato while the guy chows down a steak smothered in mushroom sauce with the works on the side." His words came out in a breathless rush.

"Like Jillian?" she asked. She instinctively knew he was probably talking about her. And Jillian definitely had the look of a finicky eater — but finicky by choice, she'd bet.

"What?" Gabe's voice sounded as though she'd caught him completely off guard.

"Aren't you and Jillian an item, as they say?"

"Is it obvious?"

Celeste nodded. "Maybe not to everyone, but it was to me. And she's Caufield's daughter, right?"

"Geez, you don't miss a thing. Who are you and what have you done with the uncomplicated, innocent cookie baker I thought I knew?" Gabe asked, his voice impossibly serious.

"I'm still here," she said softly. "So . . . ?"

"We're, um, engaged. Wedding's in June."

"Big wedding?"

"Huge. Lavish. Sickeningly extravagant."

"You could elope."

"Jillian would never miss the opportunity to plan the event of the century. Do *all* women want this much pomp and circumstance? It's unbelievable, sometimes."

Celeste shook her head. "No. All women don't, but some do. You just picked one that does. You'll get through it."

They rode in silence for several minutes. Celeste pictured Jillian's wedding gown — probably a form-fitting silk sheath that would require her to do a juice-fast the week before the wedding to make sure she could zip it up. And what would Gabe wear? she wondered. For a summer wedding — probably a formal light gray tuxedo with long tails, traditional all the way.

She snuck a glance toward Gabe, but his attention was on whatever was whizzing by outside. He'd look devastatingly attractive in light gray. His tan would look deeper. His brown curls would be a nice dark contrast. And his chocolate brown eyes would probably cause every bridesmaid to swoon, she thought.

Celeste suddenly became aware of the rise in her own temperature . . . and she swore she could feel her heartbeat pulsating between her thighs. She licked her lips, praying her sudden physical desire didn't show.

"Wasn't that our street?" Gabe asked, turning to look over his shoulder at the street sign.

"Damn." Celeste groaned. "Sorry. I'll just go around the block and park across the street." She took the next street and quickly found her way back to the address of the first winner.

"You ready?" Gabe asked, turning toward her. For a moment, she stared at him, his words ringing far too true in her ears. Then, slowly she reached her hand toward him, golden bangles sliding from her wrist to her elbow as she leaned closer. "You . . . you have a crumb . . ."

"Can't take me anywhere," Gabe whispered. This time there was no grin, only a serious, thoughtful expression on his face.

Celeste gently brushed the crumb off his chin, and watched as he lifted his hand, wrapping his fingers around hers.

She looked into his eyes for a long moment, barely breathing.

Gabe broke the silence. "I like your hands, by the way. The nail polish and all the jewelry."

"Thanks." As she pulled her hand away she forced a deep breath, hoping to clear her head. I don't want to feel like this, she told herself.

Five

"Well, that was fun," Gabe declared as he settled himself back in the passenger seat of the van. "One down, three to go."

Their first stop had been at the home of the unemployed ship builder. Gabe had stared as the burly giant of a man swept his wife into his arms and swung her around the room.

Celeste had punched his arm or he probably would have continued to stare, his mouth open in wonder. The winner had declared it was a sign that his luck would be changing, pumping Gabe's hand as if he were from Publisher's Clearinghouse.

"This next one is the fiancé of the exotic dancer," she said. "We have to deliver to the club where they both work. He's the bartender there."

Gabe raised an eyebrow in response. "Do you have a problem with going to a strip club?" he asked.

"Nah. I'm old enough to have figured out that everyone has a right to do pretty much what they want. I think that's one of the keys to happiness — if you can figure out what you love to do and then find a way to do it for a living, life is very, very good."

Gabe rubbed his chin, already stubbling with his heavy beard. Her words were true. He liked what he did well enough, but he couldn't quite say that he loved his job.

"Are you happy?" she asked, as though she could hear his thoughts. "I mean, with your job?"

"I've worked hard to get where I am and it's pretty much what I set my sights for."

"Goals can change, though," she continued. "As we get older, lots of things change." She paused a moment before continuing. "Sounds like I'm obsessing about my age, doesn't it?"

Gabe smiled. "So, you never said what form of retaliation you chose to pay back your neighbor for the birthday poster."

"Kay — my neighbor — has three young daughters and they each pick out their favorite colors of nail polish as part of an impromptu makeover experience. Kay likes the natural look and she really tries to keep her girls away from the Generation X influences. I consider it my duty to help her broaden her views a little . . ."

"Not bad." He nodded his approval. It would have been something his sisters would have thought of, he realized. Growing up the youngest of five had taught him a lot about the delicate art of seeking revenge and designing appropriate paybacks.

"Here we are." Celeste pulled into the parking lot of the dance club to deliver their next cookie bouquet.

Gabe hopped out, opened the sliding door and grabbed the floral box before Celeste walked around to the side.

She smiled her thanks. "Ready?" she asked.

Gabe grinned. He was curious to see the inside of the club, hoping the experience would not be as embarrassing as he imagined.

He held the door open and followed Celeste inside. It was dark in the club, a sharp contrast to the bright sunshine.

Several dancers on stage stopped their rehearsal to see what the disruption was at the bar, then joined the crowd that had gathered there. One of the scantily clad dancers slipped behind the counter to embrace the bartender.

Both recipients were thrilled to be recognized and acknowledged by their lovers.

As he settled into the van, Gabe looked

at Celeste. "I don't know if I can stand two weeks of this."

"Afraid it's contagious?" she asked, her eyes twinkling. She was obviously enjoying his discomfort.

"You might be right. For some reason it reminds me of growing up, and I'd forgotten how much I had put that behind me."

"What do you mean?" Celeste checked their list and pulled out of the driveway and back into traffic.

"I grew up in a big family. Our house was chaotic all the time, filled with us and every other kid from the neighborhood. Always lots of activity, lots of emotion."

"Sounds nice," Celeste commented.

"I hated it," he said. "I'm the youngest of five — two older brothers and two older sisters." His voice faded as he pictured the last family function he had attended. He used to show up regularly at birthday parties and anniversary celebrations, but lately he'd found excuses to *not* attend. A twinge of guilt followed the thought.

"And?" she prompted.

"Well, it was always so . . . noisy."

Celeste laughed. "Noisy can be good. It usually means that everyone is at least communicating. In my house, we hardly talked. My parents never argued in front of my older brother and me, and conversations were limited to approved topics: current events, school, anything that we found boring, actually."

"Just two kids?" It sounded heavenly to him. He imagined a quiet, controlled dinner table where there was enough food for everyone and conversation didn't consist mostly of yelling to be heard.

As Celeste pulled the van to a stop in front of an apartment complex, Gabe realized they were in his old neighborhood. He'd been so lost in thought that he hadn't even noticed where he was.

"Which one is this?" he asked.

Celeste reached for the clipboard to check the list. "The Mr. Mom one." Celeste looked at Gabe. "You okay?"

He nodded. "Fine. I'll get the box."

Inside the apartment, they again witnessed a very sentimental acceptance of the cookie bouquet. The lucky winner answered the door with an infant in his arms and a toddler anchored to his shin. Celeste watched in amazement as Gabe scooped the baby from his arms so the man could open the box to see the long-stemmed cookie flowers neatly arranged in a nest of tissue paper.

Celeste kept moving her gaze from Gabe

to Mr. Mom, captivated by the sight of two men so comfortable in such a domestic setting.

The toddler climbed onto her father's lap and he broke off part of a cookie for her. "She's a little shy with strangers, still," he explained, running his hand through his daughter's short blond curls. "Do you both work at the radio station?" he asked.

"I'm the new morning DJ," Gabe answered, "Gabe Freeman. Nice to meet you." He extended his hand.

"Well, we listen to your station all the time. Kind of takes my wife and me back to our younger days, ya know?"

Gabe nodded.

"You two married?" Mr. Mom asked, glancing at Celeste.

She swallowed hard. Why would he think that? "No, I'm just the —" She stopped herself. "I'm the owner of Celestial Cookies. I create the cookie bouquets for the promotion," she explained.

Her cheeks blazed. She wondered if Gabe was feeling the same embarrassment she was. When she glanced his way, though, he appeared oblivious to the question. He was happily occupied, actually cooing to the baby who had its tiny hand on Gabe's mouth.

"Well, thanks again," the winner said. "I can't wait for my other two to get home from school. They're good kids, the best."

Celeste sighed. She wasn't at all sure she would be able to stand two weeks of such sweet sentimentality. It was already making her heart ache.

Gabe gingerly handed the infant back to her father and followed Celeste out the door.

"So what's the deal?" Celeste asked as she sat in the driver's seat, waiting for Gabe to get settled.

"Huh?"

"You held that baby like it was second nature," she prompted.

Gabe avoided her eyes, flicking an imaginary speck of dirt off his pants. It had seemed so natural to hold the baby, freeing Mr. Mom so he could enjoy the moment.

"Too personal?" she asked, her voice soft, barely a whisper.

"When I was sixteen, my sister Mary moved back home for a while. Her husband was in the Navy and almost always overseas. My mom thought it would be better for her and her kids. She had just had the twins then — a boy and a girl."

"How long were they there?"

Gabe searched his memory, fuzzy pic-

74

tures of his high school years becoming clear. "I guess the twins were about six months old when she moved in, and they stayed until they were three."

"Looks to me like you must have enjoyed it," Celeste said, turning the key in the ignition.

Gabe didn't reply. He'd never shared much personal history with anyone, not even Jillian. He realized with a shock that Jillian had never really even asked about his childhood.

"Our last delivery," Celeste prompted, "is the wife of the insurance salesman." She read off the address from the clipboard.

Gabe snapped back to attention. "Turn right at the stop sign and go down three blocks and turn left."

Celeste turned and looked at him, her eyes widening.

"This is my old neighborhood," he explained with an easy grin. His nervousness transformed into a feeling of familiarity at driving on the well-known streets of his youth.

"In fact," he said. "That address belongs to my former next door neighbor."

"Why didn't you say something back at the station?" she asked, her forehead wrinkled into a slight frown.

"It's a common name," he said, "and I didn't pay attention to the addresses since you were driving."

Celeste stopped the van in front of a charming white stucco house. She followed Gabe's stare at the house next door, a two-story with an old-fashioned front porch.

Gabe retrieved their last box and stood next to the van. He seemed okay, she thought, trying to measure his mood.

"Let's go," he said cheerfully.

Ringing the doorbell for the fifth time with no response, Gabe turned to Celeste and shrugged his shoulders. "Now what?"

"Well, my first thought is to leave a note and see if we could leave the box with . . . your mom?" Celeste looked at Gabe's face. It seemed softer, even more relaxed. She'd thought he might be uncomfortable, but he just responded with another shrug of his broad shoulders, stretching the olive-colored fabric of his shirt.

"Seems logical," he said.

"Great. Lead the way." She followed him across the grass and onto the uneven stone walkway that led to the front porch of Gabe's childhood home.

It was the perfect family house, she thought. Big yard. Lots of room. A front porch where the adults could watch in shaded comfort while the kids played, she imagined.

Gabe paused at the front door, his arms clutching the box. It felt peculiar to knock, but he didn't feel comfortable just walking in — not with Celeste in tow, not to mention the fact that he was carrying a large floral box tied with a big red bow.

Celeste, probably sensing his indecision, stepped in front of him and rapped on the door.

He breathed a sigh of relief to have her take charge of the moment. In a few seconds, the door opened and his mother stood behind the screen, greeting Celeste warmly.

"Mrs. Freeman?" Celeste asked. "I'm Celeste Parker, of Celestial Cookies, and your neighbor won this cookie bouquet as part of KGLD radio's Valentine promotion. We were wondering if you might be willing to hold onto it until someone comes home. We left a note on the door to that effect."

Gabe was silent. He watched his mother listen to Celeste, then arch an eyebrow as she looked past her to catch his gaze.

"Hi, Mom."

"And Gabe is assisting with the deliveries as part of the promotion," Celeste explained.

"Small world, isn't it?" Mrs. Freeman said as she opened the screen door. "Hi, son. I've been listening to the radio all morning and thinking about calling in my own message — isn't it something that someone I know is one of the winners?"

Gabe grinned, stopping to give his mother a kiss on the cheek. She blinked in surprise and then returned his grin.

"Gabe, why don't you put that box on the dining room table for now. Can you two stay for a glass of something cold and wet? It's pretty warm out there and you must be ready for a break."

Gabe laughed easily. He had calculated it would take less than a minute before his mother would insist on either feeding them or getting them something to drink, and she had beat his estimate by at least thirty seconds.

Celeste glanced at him for approval.

He shrugged and nodded. He hoped his mother wouldn't be tempted to share embarrassing tales of childhood blunders that she would, in all her motherly wisdom, declare "cute."

Maybe this wasn't such a good idea, he wondered, beginning to have second

thoughts about putting himself in a somewhat vulnerable situation.

He watched as Celeste followed his
mother into the kitchen, pausing in the
doorway as she looked back over her
shoulder, then flashing him a soft smile.

As he placed the box on the dining room
table, he remembered countless meals surrounded by siblings and relatives, and
whoever else happened to be in the vicinity
when food was being served. Again he
tried to imagine the dinner table at
Celeste's house — quiet, controlled events
that didn't threaten to erupt in either unre-
strained laughter or spirited arguing.

"Gabe," his mother called, "won't you
join us?"

The two women were already seated at
the kitchen table, a pitcher of lemonade
between them. Celeste filled the glasses
and drank hers half-empty by the time he
sat down.

Celeste scooted her chair away from the
table. "I hate to say it," she said with a
sigh, "but I think we need some cookies to
complete this refreshment break. I have an
extra tin of gingersnaps in the van. I'll be
right back."

Gabe reached for one of the glasses of
lemonade as Celeste left the room. His

mother was staring at him, smiling that secret smile that always made him squirm — and *still* made him squirm.

"She's nice," his mother began. "Friendly. And pretty, don't you think? And she owns her own business?"

"Gourmet cookie business," Gabe said, not replying to his mother's comment about Celeste's looks. Then he waited for the inevitable next comment.

"So how are you and Jillian doing? Wedding plans going okay?"

Gabe nodded. "Fine." His voice was bland. He knew his mother didn't care much for Jillian and usually they didn't discuss her.

"We missed you last month at Estelle's birthday picnic."

"I left you a message, remember? And I sent Stella a card," he added, wincing at the white lie. He hadn't had to work. He'd actually missed the event because Jillian had asked him to accompany her on a shopping trip — insisted, he corrected himself.

Celeste returned to the kitchen and placed an open tin filled with delicate gingersnaps in the middle of the table. She immediately took one as she sat down.

Gabe's mother followed her lead, taking

a bite of the cookie as Gabe reached for the tin.

"These are wonderful, Celeste. I don't suppose you share recipes, do you?" Mrs. Freeman asked.

Celeste smiled. "Sorry, family secret actually."

"Your mother's?" she asked.

Celeste nodded. "She's a great cook," she said. "And she was kind enough to dig out all her cookbooks and notes on how she had altered recipes to make them unique, just a little more delicious, I suppose."

"So, you're close to your mother?"

Gabe groaned. "Mom, you're getting pretty personal —"

Celeste interrupted him. "It's fine. I don't mind." She felt remarkably comfortable talking with Gabe's mother. Sitting with her at the worn, wooden kitchen table made her feel as though they already knew each other, almost as if she . . . belonged.

"Well, we kind of rediscovered each other. Rekindled our friendship as adults. We had many, many years of very little communication, in fact." Celeste glanced between Gabe and his mother, looking for signs of discomfort.

"What happened to bring you two together, if you don't mind my asking?" Mrs. Freeman said.

Celeste breathed deeply, then took a swallow of lemonade. As she put down her glass, she looked at Mrs. Freeman's face. Her eyes revealed she laughed a lot; smile lines in the corners proved it, as did the creases extending from the dimples in her cheeks. Gabe had the same dimples, but only when he really smiled.

He looked like her, though his mother's short curls were now salt-and-pepper. But their eyes were exactly the same — melt-in-your-mouth chocolate.

Celeste cleared her throat. Gabe's mother seemed truly interested in what had brought her and her own mother together. Perhaps she was looking for an answer of her own, she thought, the secret to drawing children closer to their parents.

"My husband died suddenly of a heart attack about a year and a half ago." She listened to herself say the words. Her voice sounded strong, quiet. Confident for the first time, she thought.

Mrs. Freeman reached to touch her hand. "I'm so sorry."

Celeste smiled at her warm gesture. "My mother came over about a month afterwards. I was trying to pack up our loft downtown and ended up sitting in the middle of the floor crying. She had brought me a box of her chocolate chip cookies because she didn't know what else to do for me."

"Because you wouldn't let her do anything else?"

"Exactly." Celeste marveled at the older woman's shrewdness. "We cried together and really talked for the first time."

Celeste glanced toward Gabe who gently met her gaze. He was leaning forward, his elbows on the table with his hands clasped at his mouth, concealing his expression.

Celeste licked her lips and continued, returning her attention to Mrs. Freeman. "We talked about my options and she suggested I move into a rental of hers close to the beach in Coronado, so that solved one problem. Then one evening my neighbor, who runs a temp agency, gave me an aptitude test and that introduced the idea of me starting my own business."

"And Celestial Cookies was born," Mrs. Freeman interjected, smiling with obvious delight at the happy conclusion to the story.

Gabe remained silent as he drained his glass. His watch alarm sounded, disturbing the momentary silence.

"Four-thirty already? I'm supposed to be at a meeting right now." He groaned. "Sorry, Mom, we gotta go."

Celeste put the lid on the tin of cookies. "Thanks for your hospitality, Mrs. Freeman. You keep these, okay?"

As both women stood up, Gabe's mother gave Celeste a quick hug. "Nice to meet you, Celeste, and I hope to see you again. And you," she continued, wagging her finger at Gabe, "don't be a stranger. We miss seeing you."

Gabe nodded. "See you soon, Mom."

Gabe followed Celeste to the van and climbed into the passenger seat.

"Sorry about making you late," she said. "You should have said something." Her forehead wrinkled in a worried frown.

"It's not that big of a deal."

They finally pulled into the radio station lot at five o'clock. Only a half-hour late, he thought. Not too bad.

Celeste pulled abruptly on the parking brake. "Sorry again," she began.

"Don't worry about it." He was keenly aware of how utterly different he felt. He'd really enjoyed the afternoon with Celeste — witnessing the simple joy of each of the recipients of the cookie bouquets, spending unexpected time with his mother.

And he had learned more about Celeste. He glanced toward her and her gaze held him still for a moment. Part of him absolutely dreaded leaving the cozy security of her delivery van, not really wanting to walk into Jillian's stark, chrome-filled office — especially since he was late for the appointment with the caterer.

What was it about *this* woman that made him want to stay?

"Well," Celeste said, breaking the silence. "See you tomorrow."

Gabe smiled.

Six

Gabe's mood plummeted as he hurried toward Jillian's office, trying to think of an acceptable excuse for his tardiness. Rolling down and buttoning his sleeves as he walked in, he tried unsuccessfully to smooth out the stubborn wrinkles that had formed in the material. Jillian and the caterer were seated at a round table, their heads bowed over menus, talking in hushed tones.

Jillian looked up at him, a forced smile on her lips. "Hi," she said flatly, "we started without you."

"Traffic." Gabe offered his one-word excuse, all he'd been able to come up with that wouldn't require further explanation.

Jillian's gaze rose to his open neck, sans tie, and arched an eyebrow in surprise. "Where've you been?" she asked.

"Delivering cookie bouquets — so, what's the verdict on appetizers?" Gabe joined the two women at the table, pulling a chair out to sit next to Jillian. He hoped to avoid the third degree about both his belated arrival and his casual attire.

Gabe flinched as the whiny-voiced caterer listed the names of the appetizers they'd selected while he stared blindly at the menus on the table. He was glad he'd missed the first thirty minutes of discussion of which canapé or what hors d'oeuvres were fine enough — and expensive enough — for the wedding rehearsal dinner.

Jillian interrupted his thoughts. "Do you approve?"

"Whatever you think best," he said.

Jillian had selected impossible-to-pronounce delicacies he was sure he wouldn't even care for, but it didn't really matter. His tastes ran to the ordinary, much to her disappointment. We should just serve some of Celeste's cookies, he thought. They wouldn't end up tossed into the floral arrangements.

He inhaled sharply. And Celeste probably would not even think twice before saying yes, he thought. He wondered what her wedding had been like and pushed the thought away with an uncontrollable shudder. Stop thinking about her, he commanded himself.

"Gabe, we're pretty much done here unless you have anything to add," Jillian said.

He looked at her, searching her turquoise eyes for any hidden messages. She seemed happy enough, he thought and her face was shining with the triumph of orchestrating the perfect dinner. She was in her glory indeed, he thought.

"Sounds fine," he said, sitting back in the chair. It was good that she liked to do the planning, he rationalized. He sure didn't. If it was up to him, he'd take Celeste's advice and elope and spend the money on something practical — or at least on an extravagant vacation instead of the wedding-of-the-millennium.

Jillian escorted the caterer out of the office and Gabe remained at the table until she returned.

"So what's with the casual look?" she asked, rearranging some papers on her desk, deliberately not joining him at the table.

"It was warm out there," he answered simply.

"I see. Did it go well?"

"Great. The winners were delighted and everyone seemed really happy with the promotion."

"So, you don't mind doing the deliveries, then?"

Gabe paused before he answered. He realized he had actually had a marvelous time doing the deliveries — primarily due to the time spent with Celeste. Not a good answer, he told himself. "It was a pain in the neck, I suppose, but the winners seemed to like the personal touch."

Seemingly satisfied with his answer, Jillian smiled brightly. "Are we doing anything tonight?"

Gabe clenched his jaws in an involuntary response. "It's been a really long day, Jillian. I'm beat."

She didn't appear to mind, rattling off tentative plans she'd already made to meet a girlfriend at a stationery store to start looking at invitations. Gabe tuned out her chatter, distracted by the piped-in sound of Celeste's voice as the station ran one of their better commercials describing the Valentine promotion.

"Gabe, are you listening to me?" Jillian stood next to her desk in a parental stance, her hands on her slim hips.

"Sorry, I was distracted by the —"

Jillian snapped off the speaker, then walked out from behind her desk and stood behind Gabe, kneading his shoulders. "I'm sorry. I'm feeling cranky today. It just feels like forever until the wedding."

"Aren't you enjoying the planning?" Gabe asked, closing his eyes, enjoying the relaxing massage.

"I am," she said, "but it doesn't seem like you are." Her tone was clear, honest.

"It's not really a guy thing," he explained.

"I know that. But sometimes I'm just not sure you're into it at all." She waited for his answer.

Gabe's reply froze on his lips. Their getting married was a good, practical decision. He knew that. She knew that. So, why did she seem to want more from him now?

"Never mind," she said. With a quick exhalation, she abruptly stopped kneading his shoulders.

Gabe swallowed hard. Best to leave it alone. They were probably both just experiencing a case of pre-wedding cold feet.

"Well," she said. "I guess I'll see you tomorrow."

Gabe stood and turned to kiss her, momentarily forgetting her rule about no public displays of affection. Luckily, she had already stepped away from him, saving him from his faux pas.

"Bye, Jillian."

Jillian picked up her ringing phone, dismissing him with a disinterested smile and a wave. Making a quick stop at his office for his jacket and tie, Gabe ignored the blinking light on his own phone that indicated he had several voicemails waiting. All he could think about was getting out of the office, clearing his head, and ending his day.

Kay finished braiding Annie's hair and gave her a hug before shooing her out to play. She looked up at Celeste who was stirring cookie batter in an enormous glass bowl.

"Boy, I'd say you were about a million miles away."

"Huh?" Celeste stopped stirring. She'd been so lost in thought, she'd forgotten Kay was even there.

"So, did you have a good day with Gabe Freeman or a bad day?"

Celeste hesitated. "A good day — a confusing day."

"As in . . . ?"

"I don't know — it went so fast."

"Because you were having fun for a change?" Kay asked.

"Gabe is not who I thought he was. I can't figure him out."

Kay scooted her bar stool closer. "And what's wrong with people having a little mystery? You were pretty mysterious until you started talking through things and exploring your options."

Celeste threw Kay an exaggerated glare. But, she was right. And she was thankful that Kay had drawn her out, got her talking when she'd needed to sort things out. "He's easy to talk to."

"And easy to like, I'd gather."

Celeste kept her gaze on her bowl, adding a splash more vanilla. "I did find out he's engaged to someone at the office. The wedding's in June."

"Well, like they say, the good ones are either married or gay." Kay laughed and ducked when Celeste threw a walnut at her in response to her comment. "Just kidding, just kidding." She picked the nut up off the floor and tossed it in the trash can rather than launch a counterattack.

Celeste shook her head. "He's so nice. And I met his mother."

"You've got to be kidding! He takes you home to meet his mother on your first date?" Kay caught the next flying walnut with her right hand and triumphantly popped it in her mouth.

Celeste grinned. Kay knew all her hot buttons.

"Our last delivery happened to be next

door to his mother's house — the house where he grew up. The winner wasn't home so we dropped off the bouquet at his mom's."

"What's she like?" Kay asked. "Was he nice to her?"

"He gave her a kiss on the cheek when he came in and just for a split second she looked like she was going to have a coronary. I figured he was either showing off or was having a change of heart — or maybe just a weak moment. I couldn't tell."

"Was she nice to him?"

"You could tell she missed him — he's a typical busy son who doesn't talk to his mom enough."

"Sounds familiar." Kay put her hands up in mock terror of the next walnut attack.

Celeste merely raised an eyebrow and ignored her comment. "You and my mother, I believe, are co-conspirators."

"Not true," Kay declared. "Your mom's probably always been cool. You just never noticed until now."

She *was* happy she and her mother had finally found some common ground. When she'd shared her story with Gabe's mother, she'd realized she was glad to have the mother–daughter bond she'd never thought she would. She'd been the ever-faithful

93

daddy's girl all her life. Now she realized she could be both.

"Earth to Celeste . . . earth to Celeste . . . this is Kay, signing off . . . see you tomorrow."

The sound of her screen door slamming against the frame caused Celeste to look up again from her work, just as Kay turned to wave. It was amazing how mixing cookie batter had become almost like a meditation to her. It was peaceful, repetitive work that she had grown to love over the last several months.

Zen and the art of making the perfect chocolate chip cookie, she thought, smiling to herself.

Gabe forced his eyes shut. Adjusting to his new morning shift had altered his sleep habits, thoroughly confusing his body clock.

Readjusting his pillow for the umpteenth time, Gabe pulled the sheet to his chin. His bedding was typically male, broad plaid in shades of green and navy. Jillian had wrinkled her nose at his taste when she'd visited his apartment for the first time.

She had never spent the night there, preferring to be in her own environment, with her own things. He hadn't really cared, savoring the privacy and freedom of his apartment.

In six months, he would no longer live alone. Gabe's eyes flew open. He forced them closed again and concentrated on slowing his breathing.

As he noticed his muscles finally relaxing, Gabe's thoughts kept returning to the events of his day . . . and to Celeste. He remembered her dress, how lightweight and thin the material was — gauzy was the word. And her hair. Unruly waves that bounced in the breeze. Impossibly soft, dazzling mahogany brown curls that reflected sunlight so brightly he'd wished he had sunglasses when he'd walked behind her that afternoon.

And her eyes — flashing, stormy gray eyes when she'd confronted him in the sound booth. A sleepy smile crept to his lips. So, she was a widow. He imagined a faceless man helping her in the kitchen, stirring giant batches of cookies, lifting heavy trays from the oven.

He hoped the guy had appreciated Celeste, beautiful, sexy Celeste . . . he drifted off to sleep.

"You're early." Gabe *watched as Celeste dropped down in the chair in front of his desk.*

Wordlessly, she smiled, tilting her head with an unasked question.

Gabe came out from behind his desk, loosening and undoing his tie, then sliding it from around his neck. He watched as Celeste rose fluidly from the chair, smiled shyly, then took the tie from him and placed it on the desk.

He gazed into her eyes, eyes the cool color of early morning gray skies, but somehow, at the same time, soft and warm. The mark of a perfect day. She held his gaze, the corners of her lips curving more upward now in a sweet — but provocative — smile.

She backed away from him, never taking her gaze from his. He felt paralyzed, deliciously paralyzed as she closed the office door and pressed the button lock on the doorknob.

Then she glided back to him, placing her hands on his chest, standing on her tiptoes. Her full lips came closer . . . closer.

His heart thumped erratically as their lips melted together. Gabe raised his mouth from hers and once again looked into her eyes. Eyes the color of silver lightning. Eyes brimming with both tenderness and the fire of passion. He kissed her again, lingering, savoring every moment.

Shivers of delight followed her fingers as she undid his shirt buttons while they kissed; unbuttoning slowly, deliberately. His senses reeled as he felt her caressing touch on the bare skin of his chest. He craved more, needed more.

Blood pounded in his brain as he pushed gently away from her, wanting to hurry her, anxious to remove the fabric barriers between them.

He removed his shirt and watched as she unfastened the top of her filmy blue gown; watched as it slid from her creamy white shoulders and began falling in slow motion . . . finally, totally revealing her beautiful body as the silk pooled at her feet.

She stood before him and he stared boldly. His hands flexed, ready to touch her full breasts, to feel the softness of her belly against him, her thighs against his, flesh against flesh.

He removed the rest of his own clothes and she stepped toward him, stopping a moment, though, gazing at him from head to toe. Her eyes opened wide as they revealed her passion, too, increased.

His body ached for her touch. He came

to her, lifting her, carrying her to the divan. She moaned softly as he lay her down.

Then his hardened body was atop hers, his hands roaming intimately over her velvety skin as again they kissed; slow, drugging kisses that made his mind numb.

He wanted to consume her; savor her taste, her flavor. Breathlessly he pulled away. Her body arched toward him and she welcomed him into her body, her eyes imploring him to make slow, sweet love to her.

The pleasure he felt was pure and dangerous, their bodies instantly finding a common tempo. Skin to skin, they were one.

He felt himself explode in a downpour of fiery sensations. . . .

Gabe's eyes flew open and he was at once wide awake. He sat upright in bed, confused that he was awake, confused at the way he felt — and at once, remembering the dream.

He threw off his covers and made his way to the bathroom as quickly as his legs would take him, hot with embarrassment and leftover desire. He snapped on the light, grabbing a towel.

He looked at himself in the mirror, his hair mussed, his pupils dilated. In a painful moment, he realized it was a dream he was afraid to remember . . . and terrified he'd forget.

He shook his head, trying to make sense of it all. How was he supposed to get through the next two weeks when he couldn't imagine getting through another day with her?

He was in trouble.

Seven

"A special thanks to all my listeners for your great call-ins to the Valentine Loveline. Keep thinking of your special someone and call us with your personal message. Gabe Freeman, signing off, leaving you with a fifteen minute non-stop request set of your favorite love songs. Be safe out there."

Relieved his on-air day was over, Gabe stifled a yawn as he walked out to Shelly's desk, grabbed his mail, and headed back to his office. He'd tossed and turned most of the night, waking himself each time Celeste popped into his dreams.

He tugged at his tie as he walked into the room, tossing his mail into the in-basket and glancing at his phone. The message light wasn't blinking, for which he was grateful. He hoped to get at least a little work done before Celeste arrived to help pick the day's winners.

"I'm early."

Gabe spun around to see Celeste sitting

on the divan. Immediately, his forehead dampened with perspiration. He stared, recalling the details to his dream. She was wearing a sky blue off the shoulder, peasant-style dress, a silvery scarf gathering the filmy material at her waist. He could easily imagine — if she removed the scarf — if she gave the dress just the slightest tug, how it would pool at her feet . . .

"Should I come back?" she asked. "Looks like I caught you at a bad time. I just thought we might get an earlier start and —"

"No . . . no, it's fine. You just surprised me, that's all." He stared at her dress — remarkably like the dream image. Pulling a handkerchief out of his pocket, Gabe turned his back to Celeste and dabbed at his upper lip, then his forehead.

"I listened to your show this morning while I was baking," she said. "I liked what you said."

"About what?" He kept his back to her, sorting through his mail, resisting his desire to stare at her.

"The promotion. I wanted you to know I noticed you had dropped the sarcasm and wisecracks. And today, the messages seemed more genuine, more sincere — because of your attitude."

"It'll probably make our job more difficult. Too many good ones to choose from," he said, finally turning to face her.

Her smile was his reward. Sparkling gray eyes and an almost mischievous grin. "Are you ready to tackle the Loveline?" she asked.

Gabe nodded. He stopped trying to resist the feeling he'd been fighting all morning. He admitted to himself how much he was looking forward to spending the afternoon with her.

"Are you sure you don't mind?" Celeste squinted in the bright sunlight as she checked for oncoming traffic.

The week had flown by and their fifth day delivering cookie bouquets was going well.

"I don't mind a bit," Gabe said, "and as far as I can tell, we're way ahead of schedule."

Celeste peered at Gabe as though she didn't quite believe him, the corners of her eyes wrinkling as she appeared to consider his words.

"And," he added, "I don't have to be back at the office at any particular time. It's ridiculous to drop me off at the end of our day, make the trip back to your shop, and then make a delivery two blocks from the station."

"Okay, but I promise it won't take long," she assured him.

"I could use a break, anyway," he said. Besides, he was interested in seeing her shop. He imagined her surroundings would be just a trifle chaotic — even messy, perhaps, but organized just enough to keep things running smoothly.

They rode quietly, paralleling the coast for a few minutes, finally turning on a side street. Quaint cottages lined the road, modest homes that were worth a fortune because they were within blocks of the Coronado beaches.

Celeste pulled into a driveway and stopped the van.

"Your bakery is in your house?" She hadn't mentioned that, he was sure of it.

"One of my mom's rentals, remember? The biggest room in the house is the kitchen and the zoning allowed a home-based business as long as I don't actually conduct business with clients here."

Gabe stared at the tiny house. It was like something out of a fairy tale, he thought, complete with a cobblestone walk and rose-covered arbor. It even had a white picket fence.

"And how long have you lived here?"

"Over a year, now. I love it so much here. Always a breeze, close to the water but still off the beaten track."

"Nice," Gabe whispered.

"And that's where Kay and the girls live."

Gabe looked in the direction of her pointed finger. Next door was a similar, but bigger cottage that had more of a grassy front yard and much less of the flowers and shrubs that filled every inch of growing space in Celeste's front yard.

Close to the front door, Gabe noticed an ornate sundial on a marble pedestal. It sat in the center of a bed of flowers that featured every shade of pink in existence. A bent willow chair sat tucked into an area next to a tall hedge of old-fashioned tea roses that separated the yard from the property next door. A large orange tabby cat was curled up on the seat.

Celeste called softly to the cat. "Hey, Tigger." The cat opened its eyes, yawned and stretched, then hopped down to meet Celeste at the front door.

Gabe watched as the cat rubbed against her bare legs, wrapping its long tail around her ankle as it purred.

Celeste looked over her shoulder at him.

"You want to come in or stay out in the garden?"

"I'll stay out here for a while," he said. "The ocean air's awfully nice." Suddenly he didn't want to see Celeste's workplace — to see her home, he corrected himself. It felt too intimate, too personal.

"Tigger, you stay out here with Gabe." She reached down to scratch the cat's chin. "Watch out," she said, throwing Gabe a glance, "this cat will fight you for the chair."

Gabe grinned. He hadn't been around a cat since he'd left home for college. And this was one big cat, too. He walked to the willow chair and sat down.

Celeste opened the screen door, un-locked the kelly green wooden door and went inside. "Come in if you get too warm. I'll be in the kitchen, just off to the right when you come in. Bathroom's through the master bedroom at the end of the hall."

"Thanks." Gabe gazed at the expanse of greenery and flowers in the yard — a little wild and overgrown, yet it had its own unique sense of order. Tigger interrupted his thoughts by leaping onto his lap, imme-diately draping himself across his legs. The cat purred softly as Gabe absentmindedly stroked him.

No wonder Celeste seemed so happy all the time. With a little piece of paradise to work in — to *live* in — who wouldn't be content?

Tigger had adjusted his position on Gabe's lap and was contentedly kneading on his thighs, his sharp claws digging through the thin material of his slacks and finding the flesh underneath.

"Ow!"

Startled, the cat jumped down, quickly re-settling in a cool spot under the rose hedge.

Gabe stared down at the orange and white cat hairs on his pants. Surprisingly, he was unperturbed. It was a nice cat, he thought, a little too affectionate perhaps, but he'd enjoyed the feel of him on his lap. Cats were simple. They communicated their every pleasure, their every need.

Much easier to understand than women, he thought.

Celeste busied herself in the kitchen, snatching two medium sized baskets from the pantry cupboard.

Frowning, she noticed her fingers were trembling slightly and she was nauseous. She closed her eyes and leaned against the table, trying to calm herself.

She wasn't accustomed to feeling ready

to jump out of her own skin. It was uncomfortable, inappropriate, and unnecessary. Normally she felt serene in the huge kitchen. She opened her eyes and looked around the room. *Her* kitchen. She'd never thought she would feel at home in such a domestic environment, so foreign to her past life of smoke-filled conference rooms, tense business lunches, and high-powered sales meetings.

After she'd decided to quit her job, it had been an amazingly easy transition. She had especially enjoyed customizing the kitchen to her needs: huge refrigerator, two commercial-grade ovens, floor to ceiling cooling racks, shelves tailored to neatly hold her bowls and trays, and a walk-in pantry closet redesigned to house her inventory of gift baskets and goodies.

She had grown to love her kitchen, preferring to spend the majority of her time there. She had even altered the breakfast nook into a tiny office, complete with computer, desk, fax machine, and cozy sitting area beneath the bay window.

After several calming breaths, Celeste moved more slowly between the pantry and the table, arms filled with specialty items that accompanied her cookies in the gift baskets.

She double-checked the order for the unique items each customer had requested, concentrating on the task at hand.

Gabe peeked around the doorframe of the entrance to the kitchen and watched Celeste bustle around the room, filling the two baskets on the table. It was not what he'd expected.

The room was so orderly it could have appeared in a magazine featuring kitchens of the rich and famous. Everything was in place, neat, efficiently designed. A perfect setting for Celeste's business.

Not wanting to interrupt her labor, Gabe made his way down the hall in search of the bathroom. He forced his gaze away from the intimacy of Celeste's bedroom but stopped dead in his tracks as he passed a closet that took up an entire wall next to the bathroom.

The closet's louvered, folding doors were open. As he stared inside, his breath caught in his lungs. Hanging neatly on the left side of the closet were at least two dozen ladies' business suits, each shrouded in dry cleaner plastic. Coordinating tailored blouses were next, arranged according to color. On the floor leather pumps were lined up neatly, with matching handbags sitting on a shelf directly above them.

Gabe swallowed hard. Looking to the right, he saw what he was used to Celeste wearing: silky blouses, full gypsy-style skirts, gauzy dresses, dozens of scarves in every bright shade imaginable. And on the floor: strappy sandals and bright-colored flats.

Gabe reached for the doors and slid them shut. Though he wasn't sure why, he didn't want Celeste to know he had seen inside. Had he seen her secret? he wondered.

He finished using the facilities and quickly strode back to the kitchen. Celeste was just gathering the cellophane at the top of the second basket, fastening a large fabric bow at the top.

"I'm just about done," Celeste said, glancing at the clock on the wall.

"Don't worry about the time," he said. "We'll probably miss some of the bad traffic now, so it should work out just fine."

She smiled her relief, nodding. "If you'll grab one of these, we can be on our way."

Gabe took the larger of the two baskets and headed outside. The orange tabby was back on his perch and opened one sleepy eye to look up as Celeste pulled the heavy front door closed and locked it.

"I hope Tigger wasn't too much of a pest," she said.

"Not at all. Have you had him long?"

"He showed up the day I moved in, actually. He was quite thin — a stray. After a bowl of milk, he pretty much moved in."

Gabe smiled, seeing the flash of emotion in Celeste's face as she talked about the animal. "Smart cat," he said.

The mystery of Celeste was beginning to unfold in his mind. He was right. There was much more to the cookie baker than he'd allowed himself to imagine.

Gabe scrutinized the peaceful cottage as Celeste backed the van out of her narrow driveway. Picture-perfect, cozy house. Interesting front yard, complete with sleeping watch-cat. Very domestic, he thought. But what was the story behind the power suits hanging in her closet? he wondered.

"Our next stop is a business address," Celeste said. "A music store downtown called Anderson's."

Gabe looked at the clipboard, blinking at the familiar address. "Take 94 West and turn right onto Fifth," he said.

"You know this address too?" she asked.

He nodded. "I'm beginning to think that San Diego is just one big small town," he said, shaking his head. "I worked at Anderson's Music Store in high school," he added.

"And the cookie winner — Richard Anderson?"

"He was my boss."

Their intermittent conversation was limited to small talk during the mostly quiet ride downtown. As she pulled the van to a stop against the yellow delivery zone curb, Celeste turned to Gabe. "You want to stay here?" She'd sensed a certain uneasiness in him, and was puzzled by his uncharacteristic stillness.

"Are you kidding? I wouldn't miss this for the world."

Celeste frowned. Perhaps she'd misinterpreted his silence.

Gabe retrieved the last floral box from the van and stood waiting for her on the sidewalk. He stared at the display window that featured a dazzling white pearl drum set.

Celeste joined him in front of the window. "Let's go," she prompted. Suddenly she was anxious to meet his Mr. Anderson. She walked through the door, a bell tinkling their arrival. A white-haired man stood behind the counter, silver half-glasses perched on the end of his nose.

Mr. Anderson glanced up briefly. "Have a look around, folks. I'll be with you shortly." He returned his attention to the customer at the counter, placing several music books into a bag.

Celeste looked around the store. The room featured a few spinet pianos, various instruments, music books, racks of sheet music — plus all the paraphernalia musicians required. Cases were filled with portable music stands, reeds, straps, drumsticks, swabs, and metronomes.

The store was actually two large rooms with an archway connecting them, she noticed. The other side of the store featured specialty CDs and old LPs. One of the last stores of its kind to still carry records, she thought. Old, used turntables were also for sale, lined up on a shelf in the rear.

Celeste left Gabe by the door as she walked into the CD side, noticing the music titles were somewhat obsolete — jazz artists long gone, collections of blues singers' works, even albums of American folk songs.

She glanced back at Gabe. He was staring at Mr. Anderson, a slow smile spreading across his face — the kind of smile where his dimples showed.

The customer was almost finished. Celeste made her way back to the counter, joining Gabe.

"And what can I do ya for today?" Mr. Anderson asked.

"Actually," Celeste began. "We have something for you, Mr. Anderson." She placed the box on the counter in front of him.

With a glance toward Gabe, who still stood speechless behind her, she continued. "On behalf of KGLD radio, we are here to present you with this cookie bouquet as part of the radio station's Valentine's Day promotion. Someone you know, named Eloise, called in a message to the Loveline and her message was selected as one of today's winners."

Celeste watched as Mr. Anderson's face broke into a grin.

"My wife," he explained, shaking his head. He looked past Celeste then, noticing Gabe. Recognition glimmered in his eyes.

"Hi, Mr. Anderson," Gabe said softly, walking up to extend his hand.

"Gabriel Freeman," the old man whispered. "I always wondered what ever happened to you, boy."

Gabe watched as his former boss gingerly made his way out from behind the counter. His own large hand dwarfed the old man's as Mr. Anderson pumped his arm. The hand felt strangely delicate inside his own. He quickly calculated Mr. Anderson's age as somewhere past seventy, also realizing it had been over twenty years since he'd been in the store.

"How have you been, Gabriel? What have you been up to? And how's that family of yours?" Mr. Anderson's words came out in a happy rush.

"Everyone's fine."

"All married and giving your mother and father enough grandchildren, I hope?" he asked.

"Pretty much."

"So you work at this radio station, then?" Mr. Anderson continued. "Eloise listens at home — I prefer the classics and the really old stuff." His smile was warm as his glance bounced from Gabe to Celeste and back again.

Gabe gave the old man a thumbnail sketch of his career in radio, ending with his new position as morning DJ.

"So you're climbing the corporate ladder and letting all that musical talent go to waste, I see." Mr. Anderson's left eyebrow arched, then he winked at Celeste.

Gabe's heart went to his throat, hoping not to hear any reminiscing about the good old days.

"And what about you, young lady?" Mr. Anderson turned his attention to Celeste.

"I bake the cookies," she said simply, hoping he would elaborate on his remark about Gabe's musical ability.

Gabe cleared his throat. "We probably should get going —"

Celeste interrupted his words. "Was Gabe a good worker, Mr. Anderson?" She could feel Gabe's glare, but kept her gaze on the old man's face. It glowed with what seemed like paternal pride.

"He was an exceptional employee. Good with the customers. A natural salesman. Some days I bet he could've sold ice to an Eskimo, he was so good."

Gabe crossed his arms as though readying himself for what might come next.

Mr. Anderson walked toward an old spinet piano at the end of the counter. "I caught him plunking around on this very piano one evening. He's got quite an ear, you know."

Gabe inhaled audibly. He hadn't touched a keyboard in years. Hadn't even thought about it in years.

"I taught him how to read music some, but he mostly has a talent for playing by ear — composing too," Mr. Anderson added. The old man sat down and began to play a dreamy-sounding waltz. "Remember this one, Gabriel?"

Gabe stopped breathing. It was a piece of music he'd started writing in his senior year of high school, one he'd never finished.

The old man stood, then lifted the top of the bench, retrieving a crumpled, penciled-in sheet of lined staff paper. "You never came back for this," he said softly. "It's a good piece. You should finish it some day."

Eight

"So, that's your secret," Celeste said.

Both had been silent for several minutes as they headed back to the radio station.

"Huh?"

"I knew there was a secret in you. I just never would have guessed it was playing music."

Gabe kept his gaze on the scenery. He should probably change the subject, squelch the conversation before it even began. He shook his head, frustrated, but at the same time finding himself eager to talk to her.

"Too personal?" she asked, providing Gabe with an easy opportunity to end the discussion.

"I hadn't thought about Mr. Anderson or the music store in years." He sighed. "That old guy was a big influence on me — gave me a job at sixteen when no one else would, taught me the ropes. He was the only one who knew how much I wanted to work."

Celeste remained silent, occasionally glancing his way.

"He paid me well and I worked hard for him. Because of him, I was able to buy the clothes I needed to join the in crowd at school." He chuckled softly, then continued, "My wardrobe was usually hand-me-downs from my two older brothers, which I found unacceptable when I hit my sophomore year in high school."

Celeste found his gaze and nodded. "I was the opposite. My parents filled my closet with dull, preppy outfits they insisted I wear to my even more dull private school. And inside, I was dying to dress in the latest fashions. I still remember the day my mom discovered the *Cosmopolitan*s under my mattress." Her easy laughter filled the van.

Gabe nodded. "Parents are strange creatures to every teenager, I guess. Mr. Anderson seemed to understand things about me that I didn't understand about myself. He was a great mentor."

"It sure seemed to me that he genuinely cares about you."

Gabe nodded. "He's quite a talented musician himself. On weekends, we'd both stay late and sometimes he would play for me. Then he started giving me lessons after we closed on Friday nights. He told me he could have been a concert pianist, but gave it up to have a family and run the store. He always told me he had too many mouths to feed to be touring all over the country."

"You think he regrets not following his dream?"

Gabe thought for a minute, chewing absentmindedly on the ragged edge of a cuticle. "I used to," he continued. "Now, I'm not so sure. I can't help but think about all the kids he influenced over the last fifty years. How could he regret that?"

"Teachers and mentors are so important," she agreed. "The funny thing too," she added, "is that most of the time, I don't think we even recognize who they are until years later."

Celeste slowed to a stop at a red light. "I never saw my mother as a mentor until this last year. I've learned and relearned so much from her, and all I needed to do was suspend my judgmental side and really listen to what she had to say."

"I know what you mean," Gabe said softly.

"I really think the secret is to discover how to balance finding a way to contribute to society, and still have time to nurture your creativity."

Gabe looked out the window and realized they were within blocks of the radio station and, more importantly, he didn't want the conversation with Celeste to end.

"Don't go back to the station."

"What?"

"It's Friday — we've both worked hard all week. Ever been to happy hour at Craig's Crab Place? We can drop off the two baskets to your customers and be at Craig's in time for dollar margaritas. Sound tempting?"

Celeste bit her lower lip and kept her eyes glued on the traffic as she passed the driveway of the radio station. A quiet little voice inside tried to shout a warning, but she successfully stifled it. What harm would there be in enjoying a drink and a little more conversation?

Plenty, the voice whispered back to her.

The waiter skillfully emptied his tray, placing a crab cocktail in front of each of them, a basket of chips and a bowl of salsa and, finally, two salt-rimmed margarita glasses. "Anything else?" he asked, barely stopping long enough for an answer.

"We're fine, thanks." Gabe reached for his glass and raised his, signaling a toast.

Celeste reached for hers, her hand already feeling a little unsteady. Her insides felt like gelatin — a strange mixture of solid regret and quivering delight.

"A toast," Gabe began, "to the Valentine tag team."

Celeste laughed, immediately feeling more at ease. She clinked her glass against his and took several swallows from the slushy mixture.

"Hey, Gabe!" A voice bellowed from across the room.

"Hey, yourself, Charlie — how's the computer biz?" Gabe turned to wave at a man across the crowded room.

Celeste followed Gabe's gaze. Charlie was dressed in the popular corporate casual style: collarless shirt, expensive sport coat, and wrinkle-free khakis. A suitless "suit," Celeste thought, smiling to herself. Another confirmation she was glad to be out of the fast lane. The man appeared to be schmoozing a couple of clients — two empty margarita pitchers making it evident they'd been there a while. An all too familiar scene.

She looked at Gabe, his face in a forced smile, though his brown eyes sparkled when he turned toward her.

"That guy is amazing. Works eighty hours a week. Predictions are he'll be a millionaire before he's thirty-five."

Celeste searched Gabe's face. She couldn't help wondering if that was what *he* wanted. After spending five days with him, though, she doubted it. She'd watched him carefully. The more he talked, the more relaxed he'd become. And his smiles came more easily, and more of the real, dimpled ones.

"What are you thinking?" he asked quietly, his brown eyes holding her gaze.

"Wondering if Charlie's is the lifestyle you really want," she answered truthfully.

Gabe sat back in his chair, seemingly stunned at the directness of her comment.

"I guess margaritas do to you what your cookie aroma does to me," he said.

Celeste tilted her head, waiting for him to continue.

"To tell you the truth," he said, "until this week, that's exactly what I thought I wanted. Now, I'm not so sure."

Celeste reached for her glass. After a swallow for courage, she continued. "What do you want, Gabe Freeman?"

Gabe looked away. The noise level in the bar was increasing as the room filled with an eclectic mixture of surfer types and well-dressed executives. He hadn't been to Craig's in months. Jillian and he had come there once, but within minutes she had complained of getting a headache from the cheerful pandemonium that was the norm for the place.

He looked back at Celeste, watching as she nibbled at her crab, patiently waiting for his reply.

"Do I have food on my face?" she asked, bringing her napkin up to dab at her lips.

"No," he answered softly, dropping his gaze, staring at her hands. "What's with the nail polish, anyway?" He'd been dying to ask her about her mismatched bright-colored polish.

A grin brightened her face, her gray eyes widening. "It's my new addiction," she said matter-of-factly. "Much safer than most, don't you think? Certainly more accept-able . . ."

Gabe raised one eyebrow. He suspected it probably had more to do with being to-tally opposite to what her closetful of power suits dictated. Impulsively, he reached toward her hand, gently touching the nail of her pinkie finger — an impossibly pale shade of lilac, with a glittery star decal on its tip. "Star light, star bright . . ."

Suddenly, the noise in the room seemed to fade as he stared into her silvery eyes. What did *she* wish for? he wondered. He held his breath as he reached his hand a little further, touching hers gently, feeling her silky soft skin under his palm. In a graceful motion, he slid his thumb under her palm, lifting her hand so that he held all her fingers in his.

Celeste swallowed hard and held his gaze. She didn't pull her hand away, though her brain screamed its instruction to do exactly that. She glanced down at Gabe's large hand wrapped around her fingers, and allowed herself to temporarily enjoy its warmth, its strength . . . how *right* it felt.

No! her brain screamed, causing Celeste to blink hard and gently pull her hand from Gabe's. She reached for her glass and raised it for a toast.

Gabe raised his own glass, still holding her gaze, though his face was devoid of any expression.

Celeste cleared her throat. "To KGLD's successful campaign; and may you make your mark as San Diego's newest morning DJ." She hoped her words would bring him back to reality. Theirs was a business relationship, nothing more, she reminded herself.

Gabe nodded, seemingly lost in thought for a moment, then smiling an easy smile. "May the airwaves continue to be kind to me." He drained his glass and placed it on the table.

Silently, they finished eating and asked for the check as their waiter sprinted by. Their silence continued as Celeste drove back to the radio station.

"See you on Monday," Celeste said softly as Gabe climbed out of the van.

He looked at her, searching for any sign of disapproval, and saw none. He still couldn't imagine why he had reached for her hand in the bar. It was almost as though someone else had, in fact, giving his action the uneasy feeling of an out-of-body experience.

"Right," he said, "Have a good weekend." He turned away and, instead of going into the building to retrieve his coat and tie and check for voicemail messages, he walked toward his car.

Jillian stood at her office window, her arms folded against her chest as she watched Gabe get out of the Celestial Cookie van and walk to his car.

"So, you were saying?" she asked.

"When I overheard you ask Brent where Gabe was, I just thought I'd let you know I saw him at Craig's a little while ago."

She turned to scrutinize the man standing in her doorway. Keith was the latest hotshot salesman to join the troops at the station. Young. Energetic. Good-looking. He had already landed a large account, impressing her father with his ability to press past the usual "no" that the prestigious Coronado travel agency had been saying for the last year.

"Was he with someone?" she asked.

"An advertising client or a sponsor, I guess, judging on how friendly they were with each other."

Jillian suppressed any response. Instead, she tilted her head and thought a moment. "You have plans for dinner?" she asked.

"Well, I was planning on trying a new French restaurant in my neighborhood — you wouldn't care to join me, would you?" Keith put his hands in his pockets and leaned against the doorframe of Jillian's office.

Jillian smiled. "Yes, I would, as a matter of fact."

She followed Keith to the lobby, pausing a moment at the reception desk. "Oh, Shelly, would you let my father know I've gone for the day?"

Keith opened the door for Jillian, then looked over his shoulder to throw a wink back to Shelly.

"Sure, Jillian," Shelly murmured.

Celeste joined Kay on a huge boulder on the edge of the nearly deserted beach. They both sat quietly, watching Kay's daughters meticulously building a large sand castle, complete with moat and driftwood bridge.

After a fitful night — more catnapping than sleeping — Celeste had gratefully accepted Kay's invitation to join them for a morning at a favorite spot on the Coronado shoreline.

Celeste leaned back on her hands and tipped her face to the sky. The breeze was light and the February sun was comfortably warm and soothing on her bare arms. She wore a loose, flowing cotton sundress, tie-dyed in shades of blue and purple. Her hair was pulled back in a matching scrunchie, with a few escaped tendrils teasing her cheek.

Celeste breathed deeply, enjoying the feeling of the un-pressured companionship of Kay and her girls.

The entire scene was one of serenity which, in itself, helped to subdue Celeste's troubled thoughts. Kay remained silent, as though she sensed her friend's need for quiet.

"So," Kay said softly, the word scarcely

audible above the soothing sounds of the ocean. "Do you want to talk about it?"

Celeste looked at Kay. "Talk about what?"

"Whatever's bothering you so much," Kay said. "You haven't been this melancholy since I first met you. It feels like you're back in a grieving phase again — are you? Because, sometimes that happens."

Celeste was continually amazed at Kay's intuition. She was lucky to have her as a friend.

Celeste reached for Kay's hand and gave it a squeeze. "Thanks for always being here for me."

"No problem."

"I guess I'm feeling confused."

"Gabe?"

Celeste nodded. "Either I'm not reading him right or he's sending mixed messages."

"Could be both, you know," Kay said, punching her lightly in the arm.

"True," Celeste answered, "but I'm also afraid I'm the one who sent him mixed messages."

"Like what?"

"He's so easy to talk to — every afternoon has been so nice. The whole week has flown by. I've been friendly, but I haven't really thought maybe I was being too friendly."

"I'm not following you," Kay said, turning to face her. "Let's start over. How do you feel about him?"

"Business or personal?" Celeste asked.

"Business first," said Kay.

"He's good at his job. I've been listening every morning to his show while I've been working. He's kind to callers, good-natured, very likeable as far as an on-air radio personality."

"And in the office?" Kay prompted.

"People seem to like him. But he has a different persona when certain people are around."

"Like . . . ?"

"His boss, for one. Don't get me wrong, I've seen him stand up to Mr. Caufield — it just feels like he really takes his job very seriously. Maybe a little too seriously." She looked at Kay to see if her words were making sense to her.

"So what's wrong with him taking his job seriously?"

"Nothing, really. Though I keep seeing glimpses of a part of him that wants something else." Celeste shook her head. "It probably just reminds me of what I left behind — that desire to be on top, to be number one at all costs."

Kay frowned. "From other stuff you've told me, though, he doesn't really sound like that."

Celeste thought a moment. "I might be," she whispered.

"What else? What about his office romance?"

Celeste sighed. She wasn't at all sure she was ready to dig into the personal part of her feelings about Gabe. In fact, she wasn't sure she even knew what they were.

Nine

Gabe walked onto his parents' front porch and opened the door, letting himself in. He knew they would all be surprised to see him, readying himself for the onslaught of noise and raucous enthusiasm that would soon assault his ears.

As usual, Jillian had found an excuse to dismiss the importance of yet another Freeman family gathering. Finally, she'd suggested he go to the function alone if he felt he had to put in an appearance.

She had been a little chilly toward him all weekend, canceling their customary Saturday night dinner date — the first time in a year he hadn't had to dress up. She'd even implied he not plan to spend the night, professing she felt the beginnings of a migraine and had plans to go to bed early.

Gabe had quite happily conceded and spent a peaceful Saturday night alone in his sweats, watching videos and reading. When he'd called to check on her during the evening, however, her phone had been continually busy.

Maybe she'd taken it off the hook, he'd thought. Still, something felt strange. After spending several minutes theorizing why she might be in such a bad mood, he'd decided to just let it go and enjoy the rare Saturday evening on his own.

In dramatic contrast, he was about to put himself in the middle of a boisterous, typically chaotic Freeman family birthday bash. And suddenly, he wasn't at all sure he was ready for it.

He'd stopped for flowers and a birthday card for his sister, Mary, and not wanting to show up empty-handed, a case of soda. But unexpectedly, he felt just a little awkward. This was family, he reminded himself. Unconditional love and forgiveness. Breathing deeply, he let the thought sink in, admitting to himself that he'd missed his family probably as much as they had missed him over the last few years.

He vowed to find more time in his life for them, regardless of Jillian's obvious dislike for his family's rather large and rowdy festivities. Either she'd get used to them, he thought, or he'd just continue to attend solo. He wasn't going to miss any more birthdays. He was beginning to feel that life was too short to miss out on spending time with his parents and siblings.

In the kitchen, Gabe found a cooler half-filled with ice, sodas, and beer. He added a few cans to it and pulled a bottle of beer from the ice. Twisting the cap off, he took a long swallow. He hated to admit it, but he liked the taste of the inexpensive, blue collar beer that his entire family favored.

"Well, look who's here — hey, little brother! Those flowers for me?"

Gabe grinned at his sister, set his bottle on the counter, bowed formally and presented his sister with the bouquet.

"So, Mary, how old are you, anyway?" he teased. "Senior Citizen status yet?"

Mary narrowed her eyes. "Don't forget — you're only five years younger than me, brat, so you aren't very far behind."

Gabe laughed. "You want a beer?"

"Please." She turned away and opened a cupboard door below the sink to retrieve a large vase. "These are nice, Gabe. Maybe you could slip into the conversation with my unromantic husband that a woman needs to get flowers once in a while, huh?"

"Sure. So, how've you all been?" he asked, handing her a beer. "The kids doing well in school?" Gabe quickly calculated that Mary's twins were probably around twenty now. He found he had to con-sciously remind himself they were adults now. He still tended to remember them best as babies and then toddlers — when they'd lived at the house during his own teen years.

"They're both still at San Diego State. Matt's in the nursing program and Marsha can't decide if she wants to be a teacher or an actress. And she swears she's in love. I've threatened to disown her if she dares to make me a grandmother before I'm forty-five."

Gabe shook his head, shaking away the impossible picture. He also realized that when his sister was his age, she had two teenagers learning how to drive. No wonder they didn't understand his worka-holic, childless lifestyle.

"You okay?" Mary asked. "Get rid of that frown on your face, little brother, it's my birthday."

Gabe grinned at her. "Happy birthday, Mary."

"Ready to join the party?"

He nodded and followed her outside where his father was taking burgers off the grill. Most of his clan were already seated at two large picnic tables in the yard.

His father looked up, a grin brightening

his flushed face. "Perfect timing, son. You wanna take this dead cow off my hands?"

Gabe carried plates of meat to the tables, then sat down next to his mother.

"Glad you came, Gabe. No Jillian?" she asked.

Gabe threw her a sideways glance, raising one eyebrow. "Migraine." He hoped his concise reply would be enough. For the moment, he just wanted to enjoy the company of his family, pushing away all thoughts of Jillian.

Gabe fell easily into the role of son, brother, and uncle. It felt good; comfortable for the first time in a long time.

He found himself laughing easily, arguing good-naturedly with his brothers-in-law about politics and sports and, all in all, having quite an enjoyable afternoon. He was glad he'd come.

As the men moved inside to watch a game, Gabe remained outside, helping his mother clear the table and clean up. He had shooed his sister off to the hammock in honor of her birthday.

When the last trash bag had been disposed of, he and his mother sat at the kitchen table, two steaming mugs of coffee between them.

"I've enjoyed the Valentine's Day messages on your show all week," she began, "and I've been meaning to ask you something."

Gabe looked up from his coffee. "Shoot."

"You announced one of the winners as a Richard Anderson — was it the same Mr. Anderson from the music store?" she asked.

Gabe nodded. "You should have seen him, Mom. He looked the same. Well, his hair was white and he moved a little slow, but when we walked into the store, I felt like I'd just been there, you know?"

"You'll find that you feel that more and more as you get older," she said.

Gabe looked carefully at his mother's face. She was starting to look her age a little, he realized. Though her skin was still smooth and beautiful, fine wrinkles and lines were starting to show. She looked just a little tired, he decided, but content.

"I know what we need," she said. "I still have a couple of those gingersnaps left. I just can't seem to control my sweet tooth this week."

Gabe watched as his mother retrieved the cookie tin that Celeste had left behind on the day they'd stopped by the house.

Silently they both ate a cookie and sipped their coffee.

"Gabe?"

Gabe looked up, startled by the sound of his mother's voice. He had been lost in thought, thinking about Celeste with every bite of the spicy cookie; remembering her kitchen, the look of her bustling about, totally organized and . . . happy.

"Tell me about Celeste," she said.

"What do you mean?"

"There's something special about her — do you think so, too?"

Her eyes held his as he absorbed her words. "I still don't know what you mean, Mom."

"You just seemed different somehow that day you both were here. I just wondered if there was something more between you two. Do you want to talk about it?"

Gabe was stunned at her inference. Speechless. Why would his mother think there was something between him and Celeste?

"It's natural to have a little cold feet as your wedding date gets closer," she continued. "Your father almost canceled ours two months before the wedding. I knew he'd gone out with his friends one night — *all* night — and then he didn't call for a few days. Of course, I assumed the worst."

"What happened?"

"That's between your father and me,"

she said, "but the point is, you need to be sure that this is what you want."

"Jillian's good for me. We get along. She understands the demands of my job. It's the right choice for both of us."

"But does she make you laugh? Does she surprise you? Does she make you a better man just because she cares about you?"

Gabe looked away, a frown wrinkling his forehead. His mother's words were powerful . . . and unexpected.

"I just want you to be sure. Marriage is a real commitment."

"Thanks for your advice, Mom." Gabe drained his mug. "I better get going."

"Thanks for coming, dear. It meant a lot to your sister, and to your father and me."

Gabe kissed his mother's cheek and made his way through the living room. There, most of the rest of his family were on their feet, shaking their fists at the television, outraged at the referee's bad call against their team.

His father looked up and caught his eye. "Gabe's leaving," he announced, causing everyone to tear their attention away from the screen.

Gabe grinned and made the rounds, shaking hands with the men and hugging the women.

"Nice to see you, son. Bring that fiancée of yours next time. She needs to start getting used to us, you know."

Gabe nodded, knowing full well that Jillian would never grow accustomed to his family, and that he didn't really expect her to. It wasn't the kind of person she was, he thought. And he had known that going in, he reminded himself.

Jillian had been very clear about her expectations of him and their marriage. And she had been just as clear about the importance of her career and her utterly realistic views of the marriage they would have.

Gabe sighed. He'd been sitting for several moments in his car, his hands frozen on the steering wheel, not knowing where he wanted to go. He reached for the key and started the engine.

Backing out of the driveway, he headed toward the beach.

"Hey, Celeste!"

Celeste turned around, startled by Kay's voice calling her. Kay and the girls had eventually abandoned the sand castle and she had stayed behind, enjoying the solitude of the deserted beach.

Kay was jogging toward her, with someone else close behind. She couldn't quite

139

make out who, though. Too thin for Kay's boyfriend, Jack, who was a big bear of a man. Celeste's eyes widened as she finally realized that it was Gabe Freeman who trailed behind Kay.

"Look what the cat dragged in," Kay said, laughing at her own joke. "I just made a deal with Gabe, so you have to hear me out."

Celeste raised a skeptical eyebrow, her gaze bouncing between the two. "Something tells me I'm not going to like this," she said, standing to face Kay, her hands on her hips.

"Oh, come on. Jack just showed up with some tickets he won to *Cats* and you know how much I've been wanting to see it —"

"— and you need an instant baby-sitter, I suppose," Celeste said, smiling as she finished Kay's sentence.

"Right, and Gabe here said he'd be glad to keep you company," she said brightly. "We've already ordered two large pizzas, so please don't say no."

Celeste tried to glare at Kay, but only managed to make her friend laugh at her attempt. "Fine, fine," she said. "You really want to help watch her three little monsters?" she asked, turning her gaze to Gabe.

"They looked pretty tame to me," he

said, though his expression seemed as though he were not quite sure.

"Oh, they're already in love with him," Kay said, "especially Angela. They've already had their baths, so you just need to feed them and get them in their sleeping bags by eight."

Celeste nodded. "Okay." She couldn't say no, but the idea of sharing the evening with Gabe was not her idea of the perfect way to end her day, especially not after an afternoon of soul-searching. Her emotions were definitely feeling a bit raw. And, besides that, she still felt more than a little vulnerable around him.

Kay whooped her delight and spun around to head toward home. "I gotta jump in the shower," she called over her shoulder, "and try to get beautiful in the next thirty minutes. The girls are at your house watching a video."

Celeste kept her gaze on the image of Kay's running form getting smaller and smaller. Finally, she moved her stare to Gabe. He was looking out at the horizon, the last of the sun's rays reflecting in golden highlights in his dark hair. A calm smile slowly spread on his face.

"You mad?" he asked, keeping his gaze out to sea.

"Nah, the girls are easy. Mr. Disney and I never have a bit of trouble with them." She paused before she continued. "So, just happened to be in my neighborhood, Mr. Freeman?" Celeste bravely asked, still mystified by his appearance.

"We better head back to your place," he said, turning away from the sunset.

Celeste fell into place beside him and they walked silently for a few blocks. He seemed different, somehow. She snuck a look at him. He was wearing faded jeans that were worn at the knees, battered-looking running shoes, and a T-shirt emblazoned with a long-ago promotional radio event.

Compared to his meticulous fashion during the week, his appearance was surprisingly informal and relaxed. More like what normal people wore on the weekends, she thought. And his hair was sexily mussed, as though he had run his hands through it several times during the day, never once combing it, she decided.

Finally, Gabe cleared his throat. "I was at my mom's today for my sister's birthday barbecue," he said, "and found myself with an unexpected free evening. My car pointed itself toward the beach and here I am."

"Okay, I'll let that explanation fly for now, but I wish to retain the right to recall this witness at a later time," Celeste said firmly. There was definitely more to this story, she thought, but did she even want to hear it?

Celeste stopped at Kay's to check her friend's progress and get last minute details from Jack, sending Gabe to go on ahead to her house and check on the girls.

As Gabe walked up to the front door, Tigger jumped off his perch to greet him. His motor rumbled as he weaved in and out of Gabe's legs making it impossible to continue walking.

"Well, cat," he said, "what have I gotten myself into, huh?" Gabe crouched down to scratch the top of Tigger's head and then under his chin until the cat closed his eyes in bliss, his purr becoming a soft roar. What am I doing here, he wondered.

After Gabe had left his mom's house and drove around a while, he'd suddenly realized he was within blocks of Celeste's house. He'd been consumed by a strange combination of feelings — dread, delight, contentment, and finally, curiosity.

"And Tigger, my friend, don't you ever forget that even though curiosity killed the cat, satisfaction brought him back." Gabe sighed, gave Tigger one more stroke and let himself into Celeste's quaint little cottage.

As expected, the house smelled heavenly; a mouth-watering mixture of chocolate, cinnamon, and vanilla. It made him feel something — something indefinable. All week, the aroma of her cookies had made him feel weak in the knees, he'd discovered, and oddly susceptible to her and her questions.

Listening to the sounds of female giggles drifting down the hall, he suddenly felt more than a little uncertain about having agreed to help baby-sit Kay's daughters with Celeste. He closed the front door behind him, looking first to the right at the spotless kitchen.

It still amazed him — the contrast between Celeste's wild appearance and her fastidious work habits, at least where her bakery was concerned.

After first checking for the sound of Celeste's footsteps on the walk, Gabe allowed himself to look around the living room. Half the size of the kitchen, it was a cozy, comfortable room. A dark green and navy Persian rug covered most of the hardwood floor. Two wingbacked chairs were directly in front of him, decorative tapestry pillows in each one. A green leather sofa was under the small bay window, an afghan draped over its back.

Watercolor landscapes covered all the walls, and an old curio cabinet tucked into one corner, housed delicate antique glassware. Gabe walked toward the floor-to-ceiling bookshelves that nearly took up one full wall. The shelves were filled with a mixture of leather-bound classics, research books on a variety of topics, and a fair amount of popular fiction.

His eye was finally drawn to the area just beyond the shelving unit. His hand reached out to touch the dark cherrywood surface of an ancient spinet piano. The wood was highly polished, obviously well cared for.

"It's a shame it never gets played."

Gabe jumped at the sound of Celeste's soft voice. He hadn't heard her come into the room.

"Maybe you could play after the girls are off to bed."

"Maybe."

She flashed him a smile. "Jack's on his way over with the pizzas. Hope you like vegetarian."

"Sounds great," he said.

"I'll get some paper plates and napkins

and meet you in the TV room." Celeste walked into the kitchen, leaving Gabe alone in the living room.

She opened a cupboard to retrieve plates, napkins, and plastic ware. She heard the familiar beginning of *The Lion King*, one of the girls' favorites. She smiled, suddenly looking forward to the family atmosphere of kids, pizza, and . . . she paused. *A man in the house.*

Ten

As soon as she'd consumed her second piece of pizza, eight-year-old Angela affixed herself to Gabe's lap. She whispered details to him about the different animated characters to bring him up to speed and, when Simba's father met his terrible fate, buried her face in his neck.

Annie and Anessa were at Celeste's feet, already in their sleeping bags, stifling yawns and rubbing their eyes.

The clock chimed eight and Celeste glanced toward Gabe. Angela's eyes were half-closed as she cuddled against him, her head tucked under his chin. "It's time, Angela. You can finish the rest tomorrow after school, sweetie."

Angela nodded, yawned and promptly threw her arms around Gabe's neck. He expertly picked her up and set her gently in her sleeping bag. The twins were already snoring softly, favored stuffed animals snuggled against their cheeks.

Celeste stopped the video, then dimmed

the lights as Gabe walked softly out the door ahead of her. He stood in the hall, arms crossed, waiting.

Celeste closed the door and turned around, leaning her back against the dark wood. "I hope Kay and Jack had as much fun as we did tonight." A smile lit up her face.

Though Gabe knew she was trying to be sarcastic, there was a sound of truth in her words. It had been more than pleasant for him; eating pizza on the floor, watching Kay's daughters react to the story, enjoying the innocent affections of an eight-year-old.

He felt at ease, peaceful; he didn't want the evening to end.

Celeste tilted her head and brought her ear closer to the door, listening for sounds. "It's pretty quiet in there."

Gabe nodded.

"You want something to drink?" she asked.

Gabe looked at Celeste, his eyebrows raised. "I thought you might be ready to kick me out of here by now."

"I still plan to entice you to play that old piano in there. The walls are pretty thick and the sound shouldn't bother them."

"I don't know . . ."

"Kahlua and milk for a song?" she asked.

Gabe waited a moment before answering. "Okay." He stared at her easy grin and watched as Celeste made her way into the kitchen. He sighed, shaking his head. He should just go home. He knew that, but shook away the feeling anyway. A nightcap and a tune, he reasoned — then home.

As he sat down on the wooden bench in front of the piano, the wood creaked. The instrument was quite old, but in wonderful shape. He lifted the keyboard cover and tucked it away, then placed his hands on the yellowed keys.

Closing his eyes, he began to play the tune that Mr. Anderson had played at the music store, surprised he could remember it. Soon completely lost in the melody, he continued to play until he reached the section where he'd stopped writing. His hands froze.

"Does it have a name?" Celeste asked softly from her position on the couch.

Gabe turned around to look at her. Her feet were curled up underneath her and she'd pulled the afghan down onto her legs. She had let her hair down, letting it fall in waves that crept toward her flushed cheeks.

She had obviously been there a while — her drink was nearly gone.

"Untitled," he said.

"Are you going to finish it?"

Gabe swung his legs to the other side of the bench and reached for the glass that sat on the coffee table between him and Celeste. He took several sips before he answered. "I haven't thought about writing music for a very long time."

"Why not?" she asked.

Gabe stared, taking another swallow of his drink. Her voice sounded unbearably soft and kind. He shook his head. "Too busy."

"Nonsense," she scolded, her brows knitting together. "Musical talent shouldn't be taken for granted — or wasted."

"You and Mr. Anderson . . ." Gabe said. He stared at her lips that were now pouting into a serious frown.

"You don't have a piano at home, do you?"

Gabe shook his head no, and drained his glass. "I better be on my way. It was a nice evening, and the girls are great."

A small sigh escaped from between her lips as her face relaxed into a sweet smile. "It was fun having you here."

When Celeste started to lift the blanket

from her legs, Gabe held up one hand. "You stay there. I'll let myself out."

He knew better than to get any closer to her at that moment. His resolve had melted away during the evening and he didn't trust his feelings, nor his ability to resist taking her in his arms and covering her lips with his own.

He watched as Celeste nodded, biting her lower lip as though she could read his thoughts.

"Good night," she said, "see you tomorrow after your show."

Gabe inhaled and exhaled deeply, placing his glass next to hers on the table. When he leaned forward, he caught just a hint of her perfume. Lightly floral, but with a fruity essence.

Leave now, his brain shouted.

"Good night, Celeste."

The first thing she felt was his fingertip on her lips. She smiled, then nibbled on it, tasting it with the tip of her tongue.

"Keep your eyes closed," Gabe whispered.

"Why?" she asked softly, struggling to keep her eyes from blinking open.

"Humor me."

Next, she felt something round and

smooth against her lips. She inhaled, trying to distinguish the aroma, identify it.

"Guess?" he whispered.

"Definitely coated with chocolate. Too round for a strawberry. Ah . . . chocolate-covered cherry," she whispered.

"Open your mouth," he commanded.

Eyes still closed, Celeste opened her lips slightly, waiting for him to bring the sweet treat back to them. She wrapped her lips, then her teeth around the fruit and pulled it delicately from the stem that Gabe held securely.

The chocolate was dark, bittersweet, melting deliciously as she sucked on the delicacy. Finally she chewed the treat, letting the flavors mingle.

"Ready?" he asked.

"More?"

"Ready?" he asked again.

She nodded, a smile pulling at the corners of her mouth.

"Open," he commanded.

This time, he placed a piece of something against her lips — she quickly drew the morsel into her mouth. Again, chocolate. This time it was not so dark, so bittersweet. It was silky smooth, melting quickly in the heat of her mouth.

She let it dissolve slowly — the confection melted so easily.

"Truffle," she said. "Easy one," she added, her voice filled with satisfaction.

"Ready?" he asked, his voice barely audible.

This time, there was no sweet against her lips. This time, his tongue traced the soft fullness of her lips until she felt shiver upon shiver of hot desire flow through her body. She reached up to bury her fingers in the soft, curly hair at the nape of his neck, pulling him closer to her.

His lips pressed against hers, then gently covered her mouth with a kiss so sweet and tender and sexy that she felt a quiver begin to build between her thighs. When he pulled away, she whimpered, feeling weak and confused.

Then he came back to her, showering her with kisses around her lips and along her jaw, on her shoulders, her neck, her face.

Again she pulled him closer to her, imprisoning his mouth with hers. She felt transported, lighter than air and, at the same time, unable to move. She drew him to her, tugging at him until his strong hard body lay on top of hers.

She felt his hands on her bare breasts, his touch light and painfully teasing.

"I want you inside me," she whispered, *kneading her fingers into his back.*

She felt her heart racing; its beat thudding in her ears as she felt him enter her, immediately sending her spiraling into bliss. . . .

Warm sensations pulsated within her that she never wanted to end. Then the feel of him slowly faded away. She no longer felt the weight of him on her body and a tear escaped from behind her tightly closed eyes.

Celeste sat upright, the sound of knocking on her door instantly waking her. "Gabe," she whispered, immediately feeling foolish at the longing she heard in her own voice.

The quiet sound of rapping repeated. This time the door opened a crack as Kay peeked in.

"Sorry, Celeste, I know it's late — I just thought I'd see if things were okay."

Celeste drew the afghan up to her chin, stifling a yawn. "Kids were great, as usual. You can come in if you want." She sat up and patted the space next to her.

Kay's gaze fell on the two glasses on the coffee table and then the open piano.

"How was the play?" Celeste asked.

"Good," she said, "but I'll be singing

'Memories' for the rest of my life, I'm afraid."

"Where's Jack?"

"Kids okay here for the rest of the night?" Kay asked shyly.

"Of course, silly. So, tonight's the night, huh?"

Kay leaned back and stared at the ceiling. "I'm falling hard for this guy, Celeste. Do you think I'm nuts?"

"Nope. You two are my inspiration, in fact."

"Really?"

Celeste nodded. "Even after everything you went through with Curt, you still believe in love."

Kay hugged a pillow to her chest. "Jack's just so good, you know?"

"I know. He's kind. He's patient, and he's good with your girls. He's not a druggie like Curt was. He's got a good job and you won't have to worry about him spending the rent money. Kay, he's one of those true blue guys — don't you dare let him go."

Kay grinned at her. "He's great, isn't he? But what if we're not, you know, compatible in the bedroom?"

Celeste blinked. It was not a question she had expected from Kay. "I guess you'll work that out too."

"I hope so. I've never been with anyone except Curt. What if . . ." Kay's voice faded away.

"Kay, I honestly think you'll be fine. Don't dwell on the past and just concentrate on Jack. He's probably just as concerned as you are, you know."

Kay nodded. "I just want it to be right, and I guess I'm feeling a little paranoid. I really want this to work."

Celeste patted Kay's hand.

"Can I ask you something?"

"Sure," Celeste answered softly.

"How was it with you and your husband in bed? Were you happy?"

Celeste hesitated. "We were fairly compatible, I guess." She closed her eyes, taking herself back to the time when she first knew Wade. "We were both so wrapped up in our careers. Sex was truly a release — a way to get rid of some of that energy."

After a moment, Celeste cleared her throat and continued. "It all started as a hot office affair — we were together so much at work and after hours . . ."

She remembered the first time they'd made love. They were both so keyed up from working that it felt perfectly natural to seek release from each other. It wasn't until much later that she'd discovered he'd had another girlfriend at the time. It had been difficult dealing with the fact that, even though it was innocent on her part, she had taken him away from another woman. He had managed to partly convince her that it wasn't her fault, but she had lived with the pain of the reality of it anyway.

"You okay talking about this?" Kay asked softly.

"I'm fine, actually. I've thought through it and it's kind of funny; we just sort of got married because it was convenient, you know? We were both so busy and we didn't want to be a part of the office gossip. It seemed like the thing to do."

"Did you love each other?"

Celeste smiled. "When we visited my folks after the holidays that first year, my mom asked me if I was happy. I realized then that we'd gotten married because it seemed like the logical next step — happiness was not what we'd talked about."

Kay sighed loudly. "I'm sorry, but it sounds a little weird to me."

"I know. When I told my mom we had gotten married because we were good together, I knew it wasn't what she expected to hear."

"Are you sad about it now?"

Celeste thought a moment. "Not really sad. But I just can't help wondering if we had waited, would we each have found someone else to really love?"

And, she thought, what if Wade had been more honest about his family's health history and the fact that most of his male relatives seemed to have a predisposition toward early heart attacks? Would she have married him at all if she'd known? It had been difficult dealing with the tremendous guilt she'd felt when she'd discovered — after his death — what Wade hadn't told her about himself.

She couldn't help rewriting the past, sometimes. In the twenty-twenty vision of hindsight, she would have insisted he stop smoking, would have made him see the doctor more regularly, would have helped him deal with the stress, would have . . . Celeste shook her head, knowing the thoughts were ridiculous. What had happened, had happened.

"You okay, Celeste?" Kay's voice was quiet and soothing.

Celeste smiled. "The funny thing is, I really am. I still feel angry sometimes, but I just don't dwell on it anymore."

"I'm glad," Kay said.

"You better get out of here, my dear. There's a man in your house probably wondering where you've run off to. I'll even feed the girls breakfast, okay?"

Kay grinned and gave her a quick hug. "I'll come over about seven or so and share all the delightful details."

"It's a deal."

Kay quietly let herself out the front door and Celeste snuggled back under the afghan as the clock struck eleven. It had been a wonderful, yet frustrating, evening. It had been almost a magical scene — Gabe and the girls, a peaceful family-style evening, something — a long time ago — she'd imagined might happen for her someday.

Now, she wasn't so sure. Her optimism was fading. She was forty and not interested in husband-hunting, let alone starting a family at her age. And she really liked her life the way it was. Oddly, she knew she was even a little glad Wade hadn't gotten around to beefing up his life insurance before his sudden death. It had forced her to make the decisions that had created her new life. *Thanks, Wade,* she whispered to the dark.

She stared at the piano, a beam of moonlight illuminating the keys. It hadn't been played in years. Her grandmother's piano, it had always been there in the living room of the beach cottage no matter who had lived there. Celeste knew her grandmother had played, but had no real memory of hearing her play.

She got up from the couch and sat down on the piano bench, resting her fingers on the keys, remembering Gabe's song. The melody had had such a dreamy quality, something you might imagine on a meditation CD, she thought. He had talent he didn't seem aware of, talent he wasn't using. Her brows knitted into a frown.

She vowed to get him to talk about it tomorrow. She had to admit to herself how much she was looking forward to seeing him again.

The dream image of him popped into her mind and Celeste allowed herself a long luxurious moment to remember the feel of his body on hers. Even though it was something she knew she should be suppressing, not encouraging, she vividly recalled the feel of his lips on hers.

She knew she needed to be more careful, more aware of the signals she might be sending him. After all, she reminded herself, he was an engaged man, unavailable.

Eleven

"My special Valentine deserves a cookie bouquet because of so many reasons. Actually, he's in the hospital right now and I want him to know how much our sons and I miss him. He's — he's everything we have . . ."

Gabe went right into a non-stop music set after the last Loveline message of his shift. He gulped the last of his cold coffee in an unsuccessful attempt to get rid of the lump in his throat that the last message had created. The woman's voice had been quite emotional and so sincere that he pictured listeners all over San Diego reaching for tissues.

He was bone tired and more than a little cranky from lack of enough sleep. When he'd left Celeste's house, he had driven to the beach, sitting there for a long time, trying to sort out his feelings.

The only thing he was absolutely sure of was that he was definitely confused about everything. His job. Jillian. His wedding.

His life. And especially Celeste.

"Great show, today, Gabe." Mr. Caufield's jovial voice interrupted his thoughts. Both he and Jillian were standing in the doorway.

"Thanks. Listeners are sure enjoying this campaign. It was a good choice."

Mr. Caufield raised one eyebrow. "Glad you finally jumped on the bandwagon. I was hoping you would see the merits of the promotion once we got into it."

Gabe nodded, wincing slightly at the I-told-you-so tone in his future father-in-law's voice. He watched as Mr. Caufield continued on down the hallway, leaving Jillian behind.

"Hi, Jillian, your headache better?" Gabe tried to keep his voice even. Since he'd been unable to reach her the entire weekend, he still wondered if she had deliberately taken her phone off the hook to keep him speculating about her.

"I'm feeling much better, thank you. Did you have a good weekend?" She crossed her arms in front of her.

Gabe nodded, looking away from her to gather papers off the console. He resisted telling her just how wonderful his weekend had actually been. "Went to my mom's on Sunday and saw everyone."

"Boring as usual?"

Gabe hesitated. He felt annoyed at her comment, but realized that he'd probably taught her to feel that way — the way *he* used to feel about his family gatherings. "Had a good time, actually."

Jillian didn't reply.

Gabe turned toward her. "I've got to get to the sound room and pick today's winners."

"Right," she said. "I'll see you later."

He watched her walk away. Was he imagining it, or did he see a glint of disappointment in her eyes?

"You ready for week number two?" Gabe asked, dropping into the chair beside Celeste who was already waiting in the sound booth.

Celeste nodded, not trusting her voice.

Gabe expertly manned the controls and they quickly picked the day's four winners.

After about an hour, Shelly poked her head into the room, peeking around the doorframe. "Did you guys pick that last one you played at the end — where the husband was in the hospital?"

Gabe grinned. "You are such a sucker for a sob story, Shelly, but yes, we picked that one."

Shelly returned his grin. "I think it's you who's really the softy, Gabe. Here's your lunch. See ya later."

Celeste looked at Gabe. His whole demeanor was so much more relaxed, she thought, compared to their first day together. Even the way he interacted with the receptionist was friendly.

They quickly ate their sandwiches, gathered address information for the winners, and made their way out to the van.

Celeste looked at the sky, a little cloudy and just gray enough to make her wonder if they'd get a little rain. She'd brought plastic bags to protect the floral boxes just in case, though the forecast was definitely mixed.

Gabe was already belted in by the time she'd gotten the floral boxes secured and organized for delivery. She climbed in behind the wheel and turned to look at him.

His attention was on his Day-Timer planner and she took the opportunity to study him. As usual, his coat and tie were gone, his olive-striped shirt unbuttoned at the collar. He unconsciously ran his hand through his chocolate-colored curls as he made a calendar entry. Celeste licked her lips, suddenly remembering her dream, how her own fingers had been lost in his soft, wavy hair.

Gabe looked up. "We should get going. Looks like we're going to be driving all over the county today."

She nodded, fastened her seatbelt and started the van. It felt good to have him in the van with her . . . just as it had felt good to have him in her little house with her and the girls. Too good.

The cookie deliveries had gone well, and the last stop had taken them quite far east into the mountain area, to the tiny community of Pine Valley.

The weather had continued to look threatening, but the raindrops had held off until after their last delivery to an elderly couple who lived in a double-wide on an isolated piece of wooded property.

The couple looked like they were at least in their seventies, Celeste had thought, but still acted like newlyweds. The winning message had been left by the husband — a poem he'd written for his wife on their first wedding anniversary.

Filled with sugary sweet rhymes about her silken hair and his unending love for her, it had still come across as heartfelt and genuine. In person, it was easy to see that the two were meant for each other.

Gabe grinned when the old man had

punched him in the arm to tell him how the old woman just got better with age. His wife had blushed sweetly and covered her smile with a pale, wrinkled hand.

Back in the van, the raindrops began to fall heavily on the roof. Celeste backed slowly out of the long driveway, carefully maneuvering her van along the wooded lane.

"My wipers aren't handling this downpour very well," she said. "What do you say we stop for coffee — see if it lets up?"

"Sounds fine."

Celeste scanned the side of the road, watching for the café she'd noticed on the way to the couple's house.

Finally spotting it, she pulled in and parked. The building was quite rustic, built of hand-hewn logs, complete with smoke coming out of an ancient stone chimney. The place looked like it had been open for business forever.

They sat in a corner booth and ordered two house coffees. Gabe put a bag of cookie pieces on the table between them that he'd brought in from the van.

"I've put on weight since last week thanks to your blasted cookies," he said, grinning as he put two almost whole chocolate chip cookies on a paper napkin next to his steaming mug of coffee.

"You just have no discipline," she said. "Don't blame me."

They sat quietly, sipping coffee, listening to the soothing sound of the rain against the window. Celeste traced a droplet as it made its way down the pane of glass that separated them from the elements. The wind had picked up and the sound of thunder grumbled as it passed over them, more like the sound of a truck on a distant highway gearing up a big hill.

"I'm glad we stopped," Gabe said. "This is nice."

Celeste had to agree. She couldn't think of anywhere else she'd rather be. She looked at Gabe and smiled. "I keep thinking about the song you played," she began, looking for clues to tell her to continue.

"Me too," he said softly. "I was surprised I could even remember it enough to play for you. It's been so long." His voice faded and he gazed out the window.

"Can I ask you something personal?"

Gabe nodded, keeping his gaze on the rain.

"Did you ever want to do something more with music? Play professionally or teach, or at least keep composing?"

Gabe hesitated, not quite prepared with

167

an honest answer. He hadn't allowed himself to even consider doing anything permanent with his music. He remembered well the thrill of discovering he was good at it. Mr. Anderson had always said he was a natural. It just wasn't a practical thing, he'd thought.

He moved his gaze away from the window to look at her, searching Celeste's silvery gray eyes. "I set my sights on doing something more serious, I guess. When I went to college, the radio broadcasting field was something that kept me around music, but I concentrated on the business side of things."

"You think that'll be enough?" she asked.

Gabe blinked. He had never second-guessed his decision . . . until now. Now he wondered about a lot of things. "What about you?" he asked, hoping to redirect the conversation. "What's with all the power suits in your closet?"

Gabe watched the color drain from Celeste's face as her mug of coffee froze in the air on the way to her lips. Her eyes were wide open, her lips parted.

"Your closet doors were open that day we stopped at your place," he explained. "Your other life?" he asked, curious to know her secret once and for all.

Celeste brought her cup to her lips, blew gently at the surface of the steaming liquid and took a sip. "I used to work at the Danielson Agency. My husband and I were their top ad reps."

"Well, that explains why you handled yourself so well in that first sales meeting," Gabe said. Everyone in the broadcasting industry knew the go-getter reputation of the Danielson Agency. And he suddenly remembered hearing about how their number-one duo's account expertise had taken the Danielson company to the top of the advertising agency heap in San Diego as well as most of southern California. He shook his head in awe. So cookie-baking Celeste had been half of that amazing duo.

"After Wade died, I started questioning myself. Starting my own business seemed like the challenge and the comfort I needed."

Gabe envied her the feeling. To be so sure of something must be such a relief, he thought, staring down at his cup. Still, he couldn't help wondering why she still had her suits hanging in the closet. Maybe she wasn't as sure about changing her life as she appeared, he thought.

"What about you, Gabe Freeman? You

sure you're doing what you want to do?"

Gabe felt his heartbeat in his ears, a dead giveaway that she'd touched a nerve. Her question was fair, but why did it feel so threatening? And why did his life feel like it was in such turmoil all of a sudden? A part of him almost wished they'd never met. Celeste and her damn truth-serum cookies, he thought.

"I'm sorry, Gabe. Who am I to talk to you like you don't know what you're doing? I'm sorry."

Gabe looked up at her face, her gray eyes filled with remorse. He knew she wished she could take back her words, but they were words that he needed to hear. "Mr. Anderson called me during a newsbreak this morning."

Celeste blinked and raised both eyebrows at the sudden turn in their conversation.

"He wanted to thank us again for the cookie bouquet and to tell me he was putting his store on the market, in case I was interested."

"What did you say?"

"I told him the truth — that my career path was pretty much on track."

"Interesting thought, though," she said.

"Yeah, interesting." Gabe kept his hands

locked onto his cup. It would be so easy to reach across the table and take each of her hands in his. It would be so easy to just sit there at the table for the rest of the evening, he thought, order some dinner, talk about dreams and goals and wishes and. . . .

"Looks like the rain's lightening up," she said. "We better get back on the road."

A small sigh escaped from between his lips. He nodded and picked up the check. "I'll take care of this."

Celeste nodded. "I'm going to use the bathroom. Meet you outside?"

"Okay," he said, watching her walk toward the back of the room. She looked different, he'd noticed, not so gypsy-like. Her long, slim beige skirt was of some kind of natural fiber, hugging her round hips before it flared out at the hem. Instead of a peasant-style blouse, she wore a forest green turtleneck sweater and, over that, an open-weave crocheted sweater in matching green mohair yarn. Short brown leather boots completed her look.

Gabe shook his head in amazement, totally astonished that he even noticed the clothes she wore. It wasn't like him at all, he thought.

He waited just outside the door of the

café, breathing deeply. The rain had stopped and everything smelled fresh and clean. The air had just a slight crispness to it. Pine Valley was one of the few places in the San Diego area that got a little snow each winter. He imagined the old couple, snug in their double-wide, holding hands, watching the winter's first snowfall.

The pang in his heart was, unmistakably, envy.

"Smells good up here, doesn't it?" Celeste was standing beside him. "Almost smells like it could snow, don't you think?"

Gabe nodded and they made their way to the van. The rain had washed away the city dust and the angel-winged cookies on Celeste's van sparkled with a layer of fresh moisture.

Everything was clean and fresh. Pure.

Gabe was at his desk, his chair turned toward the window. More and more he found himself gazing out at the world, avoiding his voicemail messages and his overflowing in-basket. He was even more amazed that, until last week, he hadn't even realized what a wonderful view he had from his office.

"Gabe?"

The sound of Celeste's voice startled

him and he spun around in his chair, embarrassed to be caught staring out the window.

"What's up?"

"I think I left my clipboard in here earlier. Have you seen it?" Celeste walked into the room and stood in front of the desk. They shuffled papers, quickly locating the clear plastic clipboard. "I couldn't find a new account's phone number and remembered it was on my pad," she explained.

Gabe stared at her. Just having her in his office made him feel more alive. Stop it, he scolded himself.

"Nice view — what were you looking at?" she asked, moving over to the large floor to ceiling window.

"Nothing in particular," Gabe said as he rose from his chair and stood behind her.

Carefully, he leaned closer to her — close enough to feel the heat of her body as she stood silently watching the world go by. Then he slowly reached up to gently touch her hair. Red highlights sparkled in the reflected late afternoon sun. He knew he could get lost in her hair, his hands could easily bury themselves in her soft curls.

Slowly, Celeste turned away from the window to face him.

Gabe's heartbeat thudded in his ears. His gaze was locked on hers. Her gray eyes were filled with questions as she returned his stare. Hands now balled into fists at his side, it took every ounce of control to keep himself from pulling her to him to hold her close.

Suddenly, he saw fear flicker in her eyes and her gaze darted toward the doorway. Gabe looked over his shoulder just in time to see Jillian turn away and move quickly out of view.

Twelve

"You know I can't do a remote broadcast this afternoon," Gabe said. "I've got Love-line winners to pick and deliveries —"

"Dad's pulled you off that little chore." Jillian kept her gaze lowered, continuing to run a long list of numbers on the computer spreadsheets, her fingers flying on the keyboard in a blur.

Gabe stared at her bowed head. After a moment, she finally looked up at him.

"Is there a problem?" she asked, her voice neutral.

Gabe shook his head. "No, there's no problem. I just wish I would have been in on the decision."

Jillian gave him a sweet smile. "I didn't think you'd mind. Besides, your voicemail's been full every day since the promotion began — I haven't even been able to leave you a message. And Dad decided you were needed more in the office than out delivering cookies door-to-door in that ridiculous cookie-mobile."

Gabe swallowed hard. Though she hadn't mentioned it, he couldn't help wondering how long Jillian had been standing in the doorway watching him and Celeste as they'd stood in front of the window in his office the day before. From her vantage point, he realized it probably looked as though they were . . . kissing.

Jillian waited for his response, drumming her fingers on the glass desk top.

Gabe leaned against the desk, his hands on the edge of the beveled glass. "Are you okay?" he asked.

Jillian's face softened. "Fine, but I have been missing you around here."

Gabe nodded. It would probably be better if he didn't spend time with Celeste, he reasoned. It was probably for the best. "You want to get some lunch?"

"I already had some yogurt and I've got to get these numbers crunched before the one o'clock sales meeting."

"Well, I'd better check on the remote, then," Gabe said. Even to himself, his voice sounded flat. He hoped Jillian didn't notice. Her easy smile indicated she hadn't. "See you later."

Jillian returned her attention to the financial reports in front of her, seemingly unaware of him as he left the office.

"Well, you're home earlier than usual."

Celeste looked up to see Kay standing in the doorway of the kitchen. "The deliveries went pretty fast today." She pulled two trays of mini-cookies from the oven and placed them in the cooling rack.

"Everything okay?" Kay asked, her eyebrows pulling together into a frown. "Did something happen today?"

Celeste stood up straight, and looked at Kay. "Now, why would you ask me that?"

"I don't know. You're home early. You're kind of slamming things around a little — like you're mad or something."

Celeste sighed. She did feel a little frustrated, but she wasn't really angry. Shaking her head, she hung her hot-mitts on a peg next to the stove, set a timer, and sat down on one of the stools at the kitchen counter.

Kay poured herself a cup of coffee and joined her, patiently waiting for an explanation.

"They pulled Gabe away from delivering with me to the Loveline winners," Celeste said softly, reaching her hand toward her neck, finding a strand of hair to twirl and untwirl.

"They?" Kay asked.

"I have a feeling it was his fiancée, actually, though I was told it was Mr. Caufield's decision."

"Her father, right? The big boss?"

Celeste nodded.

"But why would she do that?"

Celeste hesitated. She had been asking herself that very question all day and had been unable to come up with a good answer. "I'm not really sure. She saw us . . ."

"Saw you . . . what?" Kay asked softly.

"Nothing, really." Celeste felt her face flush and put both hands on her cheeks to feel the heat. "We were just . . . looking at each other, just standing in his office by the window."

"But you think she thought something more was going on?"

Celeste nodded. "It's the only thing I can think of. It doesn't make much sense otherwise."

"Do you think you should go talk to her about it?" Kay asked.

"No. I think it's probably for the best anyway."

"What's for the best?" Kay leaned forward, her hands cradling her coffee mug.

"I think Gabe and I were enjoying each other's company too much and it's probably just better that we stopped spending time with each other." Her voice faded.

"So, why do you look so miserable?" Kay asked.

Celeste put her hands in her lap, smoothing her apron before she answered. "I miss talking to him."

"Is that all?"

Celeste looked up and nodded. "I think I just got used to having him around."

"I know the feeling," Kay said, sighing deeply. "Jack just called and has strep throat. He doesn't want the girls to get it so he's home in bed for a few days."

"And you miss him already." Celeste finished Kay's thought.

Kay grinned and nodded. "Isn't it great? I really miss him and I know I miss him and I'm glad — I sound nuts, don't I?"

"A little," Celeste said, "but in a good way." Kay's happiness bubbled over enough to make her own somber mood lighten.

"So, talk to me. Who were your winners today?" Kay asked.

"A dentist, if you can believe that — a couple of office workers and a kindergarten teacher."

"Oh, I heard that one, I think, where all the kids sang?"

Celeste nodded. "Those kids were so cute and the teacher was wonderful. They were so well behaved and so . . . so happy."

"So, you never did say how Sunday night went with Jack." Celeste watched Kay's face dissolve into a dreamy smile.

"We were both nervous, so we talked first. You were right about Jack being as concerned about it as I was."

"But it went okay?"

Kay nodded. "Better than okay. With Curt, he was always either drunk or high on something, you know? It was probably the first time I've ever had sex with someone who was sober."

"I'm glad for you," Celeste said, "for both of you."

"It was great. We talked after and things got a little serious."

Celeste stared at Kay's face. Her smile lit her entire face and there was a sensual glow in her eyes.

Kay cleared her throat. "He says he wants to marry me."

Celeste jumped up off her stool to throw her arms around Kay, then stopped. "Wait. What did you tell him?"

"Well, sensible me, I told him I had to think about it; talk to the girls. That's the plan for tonight, anyway." Kay sighed.

"They adore him and you know it," Celeste said.

"I'm scared because I want it so much," Kay said softly.

Celeste drew Kay to her again in a hug. "Follow your heart, my friend. Follow your heart."

Thirteen

"Hi, Celeste," Shelly said brightly, "I'll be right there. I just have to forward my phone to my voicemail." Shelly had been delighted when Celeste had asked her to help in picking the winners, and it helped to have another opinion when too many of the messages were so touching.

Celeste nodded as Shelly buzzed her through the door and she made her way down the hall to the sound booth.

It was the final day picking Loveline winners. Amazingly, she hadn't even run into Gabe at the station, though she'd gotten into the habit of listening to his entire broadcast each morning while she baked.

As she sat down in the familiar chair in front of the console, she sighed deeply. She had gotten used to the routine of being there and knew she would miss the environment and the pace.

"Can you believe it's been two weeks?" Shelly asked. "I can't believe how many listeners have called in. I guess love is in the air in San Diego." Shelly giggled as she put her diet soda down on the counter.

"You ready?" Celeste asked. Though she was sorry the campaign was ending, part of her was anxious to get her life back to normal. And she was weary. She hadn't slept well all week, the morning alarm beeping just as she felt she was finally settling down for the night.

"Last day, huh?"

Celeste looked up to see Jillian standing stiffly in the doorway. She cleared her throat before answering. "Shelly and I were just saying how quickly these two weeks had gone."

"Life in the fast lane," Jillian said. "By the way, we've extended the promotion, adding a trip to Hawaii that Keith just secured from a new sponsor. We're creating a KGLD listeners' favorite Loveline contest that should . . ."

"I heard the announcement on this morning's show," Celeste said matter-of-factly.

"Great. Well, here is the addendum to our agreement with Celestial Cookies, adding the prize of a monthly cookie bouquet for the rest of the year to the Grand Prize Winner. I think you'll find everything in place."

Celeste stood to take the paper from Jillian, quickly scanning it. "Looks fine. I'll sign it right now if you prefer."

Jillian held out a pen. "I'll have the check cut and mailed out tomorrow."

Celeste handed the paper and pen back to Jillian.

"It's been a pleasure doing business with you." Jillian extended her hand.

Celeste grasped it in her own, noticing how cold her touch was.

Jillian released her hand and spun around, walking quickly down the hallway.

Shelly tilted her head and grimaced. "Ice Queen," she said.

"What?" Celeste asked.

"Caufield's daughter — everyone calls her the Ice Queen." Shelly nodded toward the doorway. "Jillian doesn't deserve Gabe, if you ask me."

Celeste glanced at Shelly. "It's no one's business, really."

"But, what if a person knew she was, you know, cheating on him?"

Celeste stared, her brows knitting into a deep frown. "A person?"

"Well, me, I guess."

"Are you sure?"

Shelly reached for her soda. "I haven't said anything to anyone. I've been dying to, but I didn't know who to tell."

Celeste shook her head. She wasn't so sure she should let Shelly continue.

"I have to tell someone, Celeste, and you are the truest person I know. The new guy, Keith, is doing really well and he's been really friendly to Jillian. And last Friday night, they left together."

"What do you mean, exactly?" Celeste asked.

"I'm not sure where they went, but he sure had that look."

"What look?" Celeste asked, her stomach clenching.

"Like he was going to score, you know? Now, I don't know if they did anything, but yesterday morning when he got that trip to Hawaii donated, the Ice Queen kissed him."

"A congratulatory kiss, probably."

"Nah — didn't look like it to me. And that's what's bugging me. Gabe is a good guy and I think she's just marrying him because her dad wants her to."

"Shelly, how could you know —"

"Everyone knows. He wants her to settle down and Gabe's a good guy. Don't you think so?"

Celeste inhaled sharply. "Shelly, it doesn't matter what I think."

"Do you think it's fair for her to be kissing someone when she's engaged?" Shelly asked. "Well, I don't. But, I'm afraid to tell him."

Celeste wished with all her heart that the conversation had never happened. Her stomach was in knots and her head was starting to pound.

"Celeste, Gabe likes you. Would you tell him? Maybe she's just got cold feet because the wedding's coming up, but he deserves to know about it."

Celeste groaned.

"Please say yes, Celeste. It's not fair that he doesn't know."

Celeste sighed. Then, already filled with remorse, she nodded her head.

"Hi, Gabe." Celeste stood in the doorway of Gabe's office, her hands clasped tightly behind her back. *This is a mistake,* the voice in her head whispered.

"Celeste — how are you? How've the deliveries been going?"

When she stopped at the doorway to his office, Gabe had been sitting with his chair turned toward the window, seemingly lost in thought. She had hated to disturb his solitude, but knew it was now or never.

"Can I talk to you about something?"

she asked as she closed the door behind her.

Gabe nodded and pulled his chair back in position behind his desk. His face contorted into an expression of concern and surprise. "This looks serious — is it?"

"Shelly asked me to tell you something because she didn't feel comfortable doing it."

"Okay."

Celeste searched for the right words. *Turn around now and leave it alone,* the voice whispered.

"You want to sit down?" Gabe asked, pointing to the chair.

"No thanks, this shouldn't take long."

Gabe leaned forward, his elbows on the table and his hands clasped.

Celeste cleared her throat nervously, then took a deep breath. "Shelly told me that she saw Jillian and someone named Keith leave together on Friday night and then she saw them kissing yesterday after he secured the Hawaii trip."

The words hung in the air between them for several moments. Gabe brought his still-clasped hands to his mouth and looked away from Celeste. Finally, he stood and turned toward the window, gazing at the parking lot below.

"Keith's a real go-getter, Celeste, and it's not so unusual for people in high stress jobs to be . . . friendly to each other and happy for each other when they're doing well."

Celeste blinked, trying to absorb the meaning of Gabe's words. Didn't he even care? "So, you don't think there's a problem, then?" She heard a hint of sarcasm in her own voice, hoping that at some level Gabe was kidding.

"For one thing," he said, turning to face her, "office gossip is pretty common, especially in the radio business."

"So, you don't believe Shelly's story."

"I don't believe it's her business . . . or yours, frankly."

Celeste inhaled sharply. Perhaps it was a blessing, she thought, to see this cool, calculated side of Gabe. Perhaps he deserved the Ice Queen. "Shelly was just trying to help."

"She was just trying to gossip, if you ask me. Look, I appreciate her concern, but it's not that big of a deal."

"Okay. That's all I came in to say." Celeste turned and walked toward the door. *Just walk away,* the voice whispered. She reached for the doorknob with trembling fingers.

"Thanks, Celeste." Gabe's voice was soft.

She didn't turn around to acknowledge him, the thudding of her heart almost drowning out his words.

Gabe stood at the window for several minutes. He watched as Celeste walked to her van in the parking lot, her fuchsia silk skirt swirling around her legs from the slight breeze. Her matching peasant style blouse slipped off one shoulder as she opened the driver's side door, her silver bangled arm catching the sunlight and sending a flash of light bouncing into his eyes.

Gabe blinked. When she had stood in the doorway of his office, she had looked like the sensuous gypsy he had seen at the tollbooth that first day. Dozens of bracelets on her slender wrists, rings on every finger, bright blue nail polish, her hair down and just a little wild.

Now she was leaving, he thought, and most likely their paths would not cross again.

He watched as she carefully backed the van out of her spot and made her way toward the exit. Just before she got there, though, she slowed down and looked up toward him. It was a long moment. He knew she could see him and their gazes locked. A sad smile pushed at the corners of her lips and she raised her hand to wave at him before she put the van into gear.

Gabe shoved his hands in his pockets and clenched his teeth. What was it about her that was so damned irresistible? He was engaged to a beautiful woman, someone who understood him and the things he wanted. At least, he'd thought she understood him until he started comparing discussions with Celeste and his businesslike chats with Jillian. There was no comparison, really, he thought. It was almost as if the two women spoke different languages.

Forcing himself away from the window, Gabe sat down at his desk. He stared at his overflowing in-box and the blinking of his voice message light — symbols of his job and his life, he thought. But he liked his life. Everything made sense. Everything was well planned.

Even Jillian, he thought.

She was a good choice for him and he knew it. Gabe's hands closed into tight fists and he shook his head. He believed every word he'd said to Celeste. It *was* common for office gossip to exaggerate the actions and reactions of co-workers. He'd noticed Keith's interest in Jillian and had labeled it as typical for a new employee to want to impress the boss's daughter.

And Keith was a hustler when it came to selling — behavior that Jillian praised and rewarded. He'd landed some big accounts and had already shown signs he was a real dynamo. He would be an asset to the company if he continued on the same track.

And he'd noticed Jillian soften just a little when she spoke to Keith. He wondered. He couldn't quite bring himself to believe that she was really interested in him. It was much more likely she would instinctively manipulate Keith to want to try harder, sell more — just to please her.

Gabe stared at the phone for a moment and then picked it up, punching in Jillian's extension.

"Jillian Caufield," she said answering the phone before the second ring.

"Hi, it's me."

"Oh, Gabe, hi . . ."

"Are we still on for dinner tomorrow night at Andre's?"

"Of course, silly."

Gabe cleared his throat. "We can talk about the invitations you picked out the other day and make the final decision on the caterer for the reception."

"I've been really looking forward to a quiet, formal evening, too. Are you wearing your black suit?"

"Sure," he answered softly.

"I've got another call, so . . ."

"I'll pick you up at seven." Gabe listened to the click of the phone disconnecting. The short conversation had felt absurdly awkward. In between talk of still more wedding plans, perhaps they should spend some time clearing the air, he thought. Something just didn't feel right.

Jillian opened the door before Gabe could ring the bell. She was on her cell phone and waved him in, pointing to a glass of red wine on the dining table, then walked back to her office.

Gabe sat down and reached for the crystal glass, taking a few sips. Jillian had recently joined a wine club and had become obsessed with finding the perfect merlot. To him, they all pretty much tasted the same, but he had learned to keep his comments to himself when she poured the "inferior" selections down the kitchen drain.

Jillian finished her call and walked toward him, a black velvet shawl draped over her arm. "Would you help me with this?" she said, turning her back to him.

Gabe stood and draped the material over her shoulders. She was wearing a simple, sleeveless black silk sheath. It was plain, though it was probably created by a designer name he wouldn't recognize and undoubtedly he would be overwhelmed by its price tag.

Jillian had a knack for formal fashion, always turning heads when she entered a room. Her blond hair was pulled back into a smooth bun, every hair in place. Gabe suddenly realized he'd never seen her hair unsecured. It was always either in a bun or pulled tightly back in a gold barrette.

Impulsively, he reached up to touch her hair. "You never wear your hair down," he said.

Jillian turned around to face him. "Yes I do." She brought one hand up to smooth an imaginary stray hair back into place.

"Not to the office," he said.

"It wouldn't be appropriate or professional at the office." Her voice had a slightly sarcastic tone mixed with skepticism.

Jillian reached toward him and straightened his tie, tugging at it gently until it was more centered. She avoided his gaze as she smoothed his jacket. "I'll get my bag."

Gabe watched her walk into her bedroom. Jillian's apartment was more spacious than his, decorated in the latest materials and colors. White carpeting. Beige sofa and chairs. White material draped on brass poles at the windows instead of curtains.

There was nothing out of place. There never was.

Gabe finished his wine and took the glass into the kitchen. He felt the warmth of the wine traveling through his body, pooling in his stomach, helping dissolve the nervousness he felt.

"Gabe?"

"Coming." He sighed and stretched his neck from side to side trying to loosen the tension. It would be a pleasant evening, he rationalized. Good food. Intelligent conversation. The best table in the place. And they would run into the social elite and would see and be seen by some of the most important people in San Diego. Jillian would be in her glory, he knew.

Gabe reached to his neck and slightly loosened his tie, suddenly feeling just a little claustrophobic. He inhaled sharply, remembering his mission to clear the air — talk with Jillian about what Shelly had shared with Celeste. Before the evening ended, he knew he needed to find out the truth.

Fourteen

Gabe gazed out the window at Andre's as an airliner roared past, so close he could see the pilot's calm, deliberative face. The restaurant was atop one of San Diego's tallest buildings and was a favorite downtown destination for local celebrities, politicians, and tourists. The management was quick to separate the populations whenever they could and when Gabe glanced around the room, he saw only an extremely well-dressed clientele, attractive and slightly familiar faces.

When Gabe and Jillian had arrived, they had immediately been whisked away to the more private section of the restaurant. Even in that short distance, he had recognized several sports stars, television personalities, and a large table filled with the upper echelon of San Diego.

Unconsciously he'd reached for his tie, straightening it as he followed the maitre d' to their choice window table.

After their meal, when Jillian had gone

to the ladies room, she'd stopped to greet several people along the way. He had studied her as she'd smiled broadly, her eyes dancing as she shook the hand of a local newscaster and his wife, careful to compliment him on a news segment and her on her charming evening dress.

Gabe glanced at his watch, realizing it had taken several minutes for her to cross the room by the time she had greeted everyone she'd wanted to acknowledge. Their dessert coffees had arrived and he sipped the sweet, steaming liquid.

Dinner had been delicious, though he'd had trouble concentrating on his entree. His thoughts were unclear and jumbled, and several times he found himself simply staring out the floor-to-ceiling window, his fork frozen in mid air.

"Have the coffees been here long?"

The sound of Jillian's voice pulled his attention away from the view. "Not long," he said.

"It was a perfectly lovely evening, don't you think?"

Gabe nodded. Suddenly he found it difficult to even remember much about the evening. One thing, though, tonight Jillian had actually ordered and eaten a main dish. Every other time they'd dined at Andre's, she'd ordered a small salad and sliced fruit.

Tonight, for reasons unknown to him, she'd had an appetite.

And she seemed decidedly cheerful, chattering easily about work, her father, the latest listener ratings — everything *but* the wedding plans he had thought would dominate their conversation.

They finished their coffees in silence. Gabe knew he was procrastinating about bringing up the subject of Keith — and Shelly's comments. He hated to put a damper on the evening and anticipated Jillian's response would be heated in response to any question he might ask.

"Shall we go?" she asked, puffing her napkin down on the table.

Gabe looked up to catch their waiter's attention, paid the check and followed Jillian out of the restaurant.

They stood silently on the sidewalk as they waited for the valet to bring around his car.

The night was unusually warm and still. Jillian carried her shawl over one arm, preferring not to drape it over her shoulders.

Gabe looked at her profile — straight nose, strong chin, prominent cheekbones. She had the look of royalty, he decided. It was easy to imagine her in a high-necked Victorian gown, an elaborate wig sporting a diamond tiara.

Jillian turned, catching his stare. Her eyes held a question, though she said nothing to him.

He kept her gaze for a moment, then she turned away as though she were looking for the car.

When it arrived, Gabe opened the door for her, tipped the attendant and got in. "Do you feel like going for a drive?" he asked.

"That would be nice."

Gabe pointed his car west, in the general direction of the beach. As they drove, their silence became more thick and he rehearsed lines in his head, trying to find the perfect way to begin an almost guaranteed awkward conversation. *So, Jillian, are you in the habit of kissing all the new salesmen?* He rolled his eyes at the sound of it. *Jillian, I just need to know the truth about you and Keith.* A small sigh escaped his lips. No matter what, it all sounded juvenile.

"Did you notice Mr. Simpson in the corner booth when we left?" Jillian asked.

"What?" Gabe pulled to a stop at a traffic light, turning to look at her.

"Mr. Simpson — the owner of the travel agency that donated the trip to Hawaii?" She sounded slightly annoyed at his obvious lack of awareness.

He shook his head. "No, I didn't see him," he said, pulling away from the light.

Jillian reached toward the radio and turned it on. The soothing strains of an old Sinatra song filled the interior, and Gabe felt the pressure to try and make conversation slowly dissolve.

Instead, he concentrated on the traffic, trying to time the lights so he would hit them all on greens. When he pulled into a parking spot overlooking the ocean, it occurred to him that he hadn't been to that particular area since he was a teenager. He turned the car's engine off, but left the radio on.

The sounds of a Loveline commercial interrupted his thoughts, the car filling with his and Celeste's voice.

"Love is in the air." Celeste's musical voice rang in his ears.

"Well, something's in the air."

"Don't tell me you haven't been thinking of that special someone, Gabe Freeman — everyone's in love this time of year."

"I suppose bah-humbug is not an appropriate response —"

"Well, no. Actually, I was thinking more along the lines of roses are red, violets are blue . . ."

Gabe snapped off the radio, his head swimming with unwanted emotion. This was crazy. Why was he having such a reaction to the sound of one woman's voice?

"I can't do this."

Gabe turned toward Jillian. "I'm sorry?"

"I can't do this," she repeated softly.

Gabe held his breath for a few seconds. "Jillian, what are you talking about? Do you want to go home?" He watched as she licked her lips and turned away from him to stare through the windshield at the waves crashing on the ragged rocks.

Several moments passed as he watched her and waited. He stared at her profile, stunned as he saw a single tear make a path down her cheek until it clung, as though suspended in time, to the edge of her chin.

"What's wrong?" he asked, his voice barely a whisper. He reached for her hand, taking it in his. It was cool to his touch, and limp. She didn't turn to look at him.

Gently taking her hand back from Gabe's, Jillian reached up to wipe away the tear, then inhaled deeply.

"I can't marry you."

The words pounded in Gabe's head, followed by a jumble of sickening panic and shock. Had he heard her correctly?

"Don't say anything, okay? Just let me talk," she said. Gabe leaned back in his seat, forcing himself to focus on Jillian's face, commanding his ears to listen carefully.

"I've heard the gossip about Keith . . . and me. I assume you have too. He's just a kid, really." Her voice faded as though she needed to think a moment before continuing.

"He and I went out to dinner last Friday night. It was fun to talk to someone new. He's lived all over the world and I found myself getting lost in his stories about Paris and Rome and . . ."

Gabe focused on Jillian's mouth, watching her lips as she formed the words.

"Nothing's happened between us, first of all. What *did* happen, though, was that somewhere during that evening, I discovered I wasn't really sure about myself — or sure about us." She glanced briefly toward him, then looked down at her hands.

"What do you mean?" he asked.

"When I used to think about how the rest of our life was going to be after we were married, I used to feel so safe and secure — and that it was *exactly* what I

201

wanted. Now it's almost as though I've tasted of something — something I want more of."

"Keith?"

Jillian bit her lower lip before answering him. "I saw you reaching for Celeste the other afternoon and I realized that I wasn't even angry or jealous — all I felt was . . . territorial."

Gabe nodded. She *had* thought something more was happening.

"I've thought about this a long time, and I realized that I haven't been fair to either you or me. Daddy is right — you are a great catch for me and I know he wants me to settle down."

"He loves you."

"I know. But, he hasn't taught me about love, you know?" Another tear made a path down her cheek.

Gabe reached into his pocket and handed her a handkerchief. She gave him a sweet smile as she dabbed at her eyes.

"What I'm trying to say is that I want the kind of attraction to a man that I see in your eyes when you look at Celeste."

"I haven't —"

"I know, I know. It's nothing you have any control over. That's the part that I've been thinking about. And it's the part that we each deserve, don't we?"

Gabe closed his eyes. He had thought it wasn't detectable. He had tried so hard to hide his emotions, but obviously hadn't succeeded, at least with Jillian.

"Gabe, at first I thought all those Valentine messages from the Loveline were trite and foolish. Now, I'm not so sure. I honestly didn't think any of it was real, and now all I can think about is finding a way to experience the kinds of feelings that all those callers kept talking about."

"So, what do you want to do?" Gabe asked, his voice soft and quiet.

Jillian turned to him, relief shining in her face. "I want to tell you how much I care about you and tell *you* to follow your heart. I'm grateful to have learned this much already. And I'm going to be just fine, I can feel it."

Gabe stared into her misty eyes. Her face had relaxed considerably and there was a smile forming behind her tears. He shook his head, unable to find the right words to respond to her.

Jillian reached for him, laying her hand on his cheek. "Will you laugh if I tell you I hope we can still be friends?"

Gabe smiled. "Sounds funny, though, doesn't it?"

Jillian nodded. "But, I really mean it," she whispered.

"I think we could work on it," he said.

Jillian sighed. "I know this evening didn't end the way you thought it would —"

"What about the invitations and the —"

"I canceled them yesterday. Everything's canceled. Now I just have to tell Daddy." She groaned and looked away.

"Just tell him exactly like you told me. I bet you'll be surprised at how understanding he'll be."

"I hope so — he's losing all the deposit money he put down everywhere." Her chuckle was dry and forced.

Almost out of habit, Gabe winced. He knew in the end, though, Mr. Caufield would want the best for his daughter. And he had a feeling he would understand her desire for true love, for true happiness.

"Oh, Gabe," she said, her voice sounding uncharacteristically wistful. "You and I have had quite a journey, haven't we?"

Gabe nodded, turning the key in the ignition. Somehow, he had the distinct feeling that the journey was just beginning for Jillian and for him.

Gabe sat in his car as he watched Jillian walk toward the doorman of her apartment building. Her step seemed light and care-free. He hoped she felt like he did, that a huge weight had been lifted. Just before she reached the door, Jillian turned toward him, smiled and blew him a kiss. The smile was different, one he'd never seen before. She would be fine, he thought.

Drumming his fingers on the steering wheel, Gabe battled for a moment with the tremendous feeling of restlessness that threatened to overwhelm him. He should be dead-tired after the evening he'd just had. Instead, he felt like he used to feel getting ready to work the graveyard shift. He felt energized.

Rather than fight with insomnia, Gabe backed out of his parking spot and headed toward the radio station. There, he could at least feel functional, useful. He could at-tack the mound of paperwork, empty his voicemail, and have a clean desk to greet him on Monday morning for a change.

As Gabe parked near the door, he had a comforting feeling of déjà vu. It was like old times — when things were simpler, not so complicated. He let himself in and walked down the hall, stopping a moment to wave to the graveyard shift DJ who had replaced his position when he'd moved to days.

After a peaceful, uninterrupted hour,

most of his paperwork was done and the voicemail light was no longer blinking. An interoffice line rang loudly, startling him. He punched the speaker button.

"Gabe Freeman."

"Hey, Gabe."

"Hey, yourself, Greg. Sounds like you're having a good night."

"Miss your old shift, huh?"

"Not a bit. Just had some free time and thought I'd take advantage of my insomnia."

Greg chuckled softly. "Old habits die hard, don't they?"

"I guess."

"Gabe, as long as you're here, you want to do me a favor and look for the tapes of the new Loveline spots? I can't find them in here and I bet they're in the sound booth."

"Sure. Be right there." Gabe punched the speaker button off,

In the sound booth, Gabe located the missing tapes. Greg gave him a thumbs up as he reached for them, continuing his smooth adlibbing on the air. Greg had a breathless, sexy on-air voice that served him well on the night shift. He had gladly jumped from a rival station when the position had become available. Gabe liked him.

He was young and ambitious, and loved the business.

He had to admit that Greg reminded him a little of himself. He grimaced. Now he wasn't sure how he felt about the radio business, or anything else, for that matter.

Walking back into the sound booth, Gabe started straightening the stacks of tapes he'd disturbed looking for the tape for Greg. When he looked down, he realized his hand was resting on the first versions of the Loveline commercials that he and Celeste had recorded at the beginning of the promotion.

Impulsively, he popped in the cassette. The first thing he heard was Celeste's musical laughter. It rang in his ears and compelled him to sit down. That first recording session, he remembered, was more like outtakes — radio bloopers, he thought. With just Celeste and Brent and him in the booth, he'd thought they'd never get through the session with anything worth airing.

"And what is this thing called love?" Celeste asked, audibly stifling a giggle. "I'm sorry, I'm sorry." Her laughter escaped and infected the whole group until they were all laughing.

"Are you going to be able to do this or

not?" Gabe asked, feigned irritation in his voice.

"I'm trying, honestly," she said, fresh laughter coloring her voice.

Brent's voice jumped in. "Do you want to rehearse some more, Celeste? No? Okay, let's try this again." Brent's voice sounded patient, as though he was quite unconcerned about the delay the retakes were causing. "Celeste — you ready now?"

"Let's do it," she said. She cleared her throat. "And what is this thing called love?"

"You're not going to make me count the ways, are you?" Gabe's voice had a definite teasing quality.

"No, silly, just tell me . . . one way." Celeste's voice had a low, sultry tone.

"Perfect," Brent said. "We'll use that one and add the contest details later. Let's keep going. Okay, Gabe, you're up."

He cleared his throat. "Wondering about Valentine's Day? Do something different this year for the one you dream about. Tell all of San Diego how you really feel about the one you love. Call KGLD's Loveline . . . bare your soul . . . expose your heart. Tell us about your . . . special Valentine."

There was a pause of silence, then Brent's voice. "One-take Freeman. That was impeccable, Gabe. Good tone, lots of emotion, said like you meant it, man."

Gabe hit the stop button on the tape. He closed his eyes, picturing that day. Celeste in her preposterous skirt made out of neckties, her bracelets jingling so much that she'd had to remove them during the recording, how her blouse kept slipping off her shoulder exposing pale, creamy skin.

It had been fun, he admitted. Their chemistry came through on the recordings and had indeed served to draw KGLD listeners to pick up the phone. It had been the best promotion the station had ever produced, and their ratings had gone through the roof during the two weeks.

Gabe rubbed his eyes, suddenly feeling the fatigue he'd been suppressing. He yawned and made his way to his office. He laid down on the sofa and closed his eyes, the sweet sound of Celeste's laughter still ringing in his ears.

Celeste threw her covers to the foot of the bed. The night had been still and unseasonally warm, with no cooling ocean breezes to soothe her restlessness.

"This is ridiculous," she said out loud to the dark. "I might as well just get up and get something productive done." She flipped on her bedside lamp and looked at the clock. She guessed she'd gotten about two hours of sleep throughout the night, between the heat and her own tossing and turning. The sun would be up in about an hour, she thought, so she might as well just start the day.

She took a lukewarm shower and slipped into a loose cotton sundress. As she made her way toward the kitchen, the hardwood floors chilled her bare feet.

Her goal for the morning was to make final adjustments to the peanut butter chip cookie recipe she'd been working on in order to add it to the choices she intended to list in her next newspaper advertisement. It was almost there, but something was missing.

After a cup of coffee and a bran muffin, Celeste easily fell into the comfortable routine of reaching for bowls and spoons and measuring cups, checking her notes carefully as she gathered ingredients.

A sound distracted her from her notes and she looked up for a moment, tipping her head to listen. Tigger jumped onto the ledge outside the kitchen window and yowled pitifully.

"By the sound of your voice," she said, "anyone would think you were starving to death." She put down the bottle of vanilla and went to the front door.

Tigger was patiently waiting on the front step when she opened the door, his purr starting the moment he saw her.

Celeste reached down to scratch his head and he flopped down on his side, stretching his long body in cat ecstasy. "Come on in, lazy cat, and have some breakfast."

Celeste turned and Tigger jumped to his feet to follow her. She shook some dry food into his bowl and set it on the floor. With the background sound of the soft crunching of cat food, Celeste poured herself a second cup of coffee and sat on the bench next to the kitchen's bay window.

The sun was just coming up and the sky was a pale pink, completely devoid of clouds. "Looks like another warm day today, Tigger. Better get the baking done early."

Bowl now empty, Tigger jumped up on the window bench next to Celeste, climbing into her lap. He lowered his head and pushed it against her hand, demanding attention.

"Okay, okay." She rubbed his cheeks and scratched under his chin. His purr rumbled louder as she ran her hands along his back reaching to the tip of his tail.

Suddenly, he yowled and jumped down from her lap, turning around as though he was waiting for her to follow him.

"Okay, I'm coming." Celeste walked to the front door where the cat was standing on his hind legs, his front paws stretching upward to rest on the door. He meowed softly and continued purring until she opened the door.

"Do we have a visitor, huh? At this hour?" Celeste opened the door and Tigger slipped out to run toward the fence.

Gabe's car was parked at the curb and he was leaning against it, his arms folded against his chest.

Fifteen

Celeste stood in the doorway as she watched Tigger scamper across the front yard toward the street and squeeze through the white picket fence. There, he rubbed against Gabe's legs until he succumbed and reached down to pet him.

Gabe scratched Tigger's head and finally picked him up, cradling him in his arms. "He's a pretty good watch cat," Gabe said as he nudged open the gate with his hip and walked toward Celeste.

He was dressed in black pants and white shirt, sleeves rolled up to just below his elbows. Although he looked a little rumpled, he seemed rather relaxed — certainly not like anything was wrong, she thought. But, what was he doing at her house in the wee hours of the morning?

Gabe stopped, standing in front of her on the sidewalk, still stroking the cat in his arms.

"Just out for a stroll in my neighborhood?" she asked.

"Kind of. Had a rough night."

She should just send him on his way. She knew that. "Want some coffee?"

His grin instantly melted her resolve and Celeste quickly turned away, hoping he didn't see how much his smile affected her.

"And cookies?" he asked.

Celeste turned her head back to look at him as she walked into the house. "I always have cookies."

Tigger jumped down from Gabe's arms to retreat to his garden chair perch as Gabe followed Celeste into the house. As he walked into the kitchen, a wonderful aroma assaulted his senses immediately. Just what he didn't need: damn truth-serum cookies.

Celeste handed Gabe an oversized mug of coffee and he took a sip, fragrant steam causing him to close his eyes for a moment. It felt so right to be there with her, he thought. Very right.

Celeste washed and dried her hands at the large stainless steel double sink, then grabbed a half-apron from a hook on the wall. "Okay if I keep working? I've got both ovens preheated and I need to finish four more batches before the day gets too warm."

"Sure. Can I lend a hand?" Gabe

214

watched her for a moment as she continued gathering supplies, amazed at the amount of ingredients already waiting on the butcher block table in the middle of the room.

"You want to wash up first?" Celeste nodded toward the hallway and smiled.

Gabe turned to make his way toward the bathroom. As he walked into Celeste's bedroom he stopped abruptly in front of the closet, staring at the huge empty space there. Where once were a dozen business suits, only naked, empty hangers now hung.

He reached to the floor of the closet to pick up a scarf that had fallen, briefly bringing it to his face. He breathed the scent of her — an irresistible, indescribable mixture of sweetness.

He should go home. Everything in his logical brain knew that, but as he carefully placed the scarf with the rest of the riot of silk that hung there, Gabe knew he was going to stay.

Celeste stood in the middle of the kitchen, leaning heavily on the counter with both hands, her heartbeat pounding in her ears. How could he look so adorable at this hour of the day?

She breathed deeply and looked around

the kitchen, soon busying herself dumping ingredients into an oversized ceramic bowl. She looked up at the sound of footsteps.

"What can I do?" Gabe asked.

Celeste handed him a well-worn wooden spoon. "Stir." Gabe looked at the huge bowl on the counter. He held one side and began to carefully stir the ingredients, concentrating on keeping the flour from spilling over the sides.

"It'll be easier if you slow down a little," she said, "and move things around like this." Celeste took the wooden spoon from him and demonstrated how to scoop and pull the ingredients together rather than force them using rough circular motions.

"Got it," he replied. Gabe mimicked her movements, pausing each time she added more ingredients.

"Okay, stop," she said softly, placing her hand on his. "It's better not to over-mix." Her heart skipped a beat as she looked into his chocolate brown eyes for a long moment. What was he feeling? And why was he standing in her kitchen in formal clothes that were quickly being dusted with cinnamon and flour?

They continued working in silence, dropping tablespoon-sized lumps of cookie dough onto shiny stainless steel sheets.

When they were finished, Celeste put the cookie sheets into both ovens and set the timer.

Gabe reached for his coffee mug and sat on a stool at the counter, watching Celeste as she worked.

She soon joined him, placing two small plates of cookie pieces on the counter between them. "These are two different batches — tell me which one you like better."

Gabe grinned at her. "It's a tough job, but somebody's got to do it, right?" he quipped.

"Let's just see how discriminating you really are," she said, popping a morsel into her mouth.

Gabe selected a large piece, put it into his mouth and chewed, closing his eyes as if to concentrate on the taste.

Celeste stared at him while he chewed. His face was darkened by the growth of his heavy beard and one side of his hair was flatter, she noticed as though he'd been sleeping on one side. While he chewed, she watched the creases at the corner of his eyes crinkle with the movement of his jaws. Her gaze dropped to his cheeks, dimples already threatening to appear.

Eyes still closed, Gabe brought his mug

to his lips. "Now to cleanse the palate," he said, licking his lips. Then he held his hand out blindly over the counter. "The other cookie, please."

She shook her head and selected a piece from the other plate and placed it in the palm of his hand. He put it in his mouth and chewed. His eyebrows raised a little, then his brow furrowed.

Gabe opened his eyes and looked at the plates of cookie nieces. "They look the same, but there's something different about that second piece. It was more buttery or something." He took another piece from the second plate.

Celeste watched, amused at his concentration.

"Peanut butter? Is that what I taste?"

Celeste nodded. "My friend Brian gave me his recipe — a chocolate chip cookie with peanut butter chips added. I'm very impressed, Mr. Freeman, at your talent for cookie tasting."

Gabe smiled. "Maybe I should be really sure," he said, reaching for another piece.

The chiming of the timer interrupted Celeste from commenting and she went to the ovens, carefully removing the cookie sheets and placing them in the tall cooling racks.

"Ready for another batch?" she asked.

Gabe gave her a small salute and stood up, still chewing his last cookie piece.

Celeste reached for a long chef's apron from the wall. "You'd better put this on — your slacks are looking pretty dusty."

Gabe looked down at the flour smudges on his thighs.

"Come here," she said. Gabe obediently stood in front of Celeste as she stood up on tiptoes to put the apron's neck loop over his head, then stepped behind him to cross the long waist straps as he held his arms up. Without thinking, she stepped close to him and took each end around to the front, intending to cross the long straps again before bringing them to the back to knot.

As her arms extended on either side of Gabe's waist, Celeste suddenly realized what an intimate position they were in. She froze, her cheek dangerously close to nuzzling against his back, her hands suspended in front of him.

Then she felt his hands encircle her wrists, gently drawing her arms against him until they were wrapped tightly around his waist. She felt her breathing become instantly ragged. The feel of his hard body against her arms sent her pulse racing.

Gabe pulled her tighter until her body rested against his and she gave in, nestling her cheek against the hollow between his shoulder blades. He felt warm and strong and solid. She closed her eyes, ignoring every impulse to pull away from him.

"Celeste?" Gabe whispered.

Celeste had no control over her voice. She inhaled deeply, knowing the precious moment would end if she spoke.

"Celeste, I can't help the way I feel about you. I tried, believe me, but it took Jillian to point out that it was hopeless. The wedding is off."

Celeste's eyes snapped open. *The wedding was off?*

Gabe loosened his hold on her arms, dropping them just long enough to turn around, reaching for her again when he faced her.

Celeste stood still, her arms limp at her sides and Gabe's hands now gently cupping her shoulders. She gazed into his eyes until she thought she might get lost in them.

"Did you hear me?" he asked softly, his eyes searching hers.

She nodded, still speechless, and watched as he leaned toward her, his eyes filled with tenderness. Focusing on his mouth, she watched as he came closer, closer.

"Do you want me to stop?" he whispered, lifting his chin, brushing a gentle kiss on her forehead.

Celeste lifted her hands and wrapped them around his waist to pull him to her. Then she felt his open hand on the small of her back, pressing her to him. It felt so good to be so close, she thought, amazed that they were standing in the middle of her kitchen with their arms around each other.

After several moments, reluctantly, they parted a few inches, her body still tingling from the contact.

"I want to kiss you," he whispered, his breath hot against her ear.

She felt his lips next to her ear, then his prickly cheek rubbing against her cheek as he seared a path of kisses to her lips, finally bringing his mouth to hers in a gentle, slow kiss.

She drank in its sweetness. Shivers of delight ran through her as their bodies came even closer together. The blood pounded in her brain and her knees trembled as she became lost — the caress of his kiss setting her body aflame.

Limp in his embrace, she felt him sweep her effortlessly into his arms, lifting her off her feet. "Wait," she murmured. "The ovens . . ."

He carried her toward the ovens and tilted her toward them just long enough for her to turn off the heat.

Then she buried her face against his throat as he swung her around toward the doorway. "Are you sure I'm not too heavy —"

"Don't get me started about women and their weight," he warned, squeezing her gently against him.

Celeste felt her soft curves molding to the contours of Gabe's chest as he carried her into the bedroom, settling her gently on her bed. He sat on the edge, gazing at her as if waiting for her direction.

"Come here," she whispered, her eyes half-closed.

He leaned toward her until his breath softly fanned her face. She reached her hands up until her fingers were buried in his thick hair, pulling him to her until his lips pressed once again against hers. Long, delicious moments later he pulled away from her, kissing the pulsing hollow at the base of her throat.

She reached for his hand and moved it to her breast, holding it there, and holding his gaze.

A low moan escaped from Gabe's throat as he gently massaged her breast, running his thumb against her nipple until it hardened, watching the desire build in her eyes. A soft moan escaped her lips.

"I think we need to get out of our . . . aprons," he whispered, gazing at the broad smile that lit her face.

They quickly helped each other out of their clothes, their pace quickening as each inch of skin was exposed.

"You are so beautiful," he whispered, gently tumbling her back down on the bed. His hand cupped her chin then slid gently down her neck and arm. His hands moved slowly across her silken belly and back up to her breasts. He lowered his mouth to her swollen nipples, sucking and teasing until he felt her hands on his shoulders, pulling his body to hers.

"Gabe," she whispered, pulling at his body until he lay on top of hers. All she could think about was feeling him inside her. All she wanted was to be released from the hungry desire that consumed her. She reached for him and felt him shudder when she squeezed his hardness in the palm of her hand.

"Condom?" he asked breathlessly, pulling slightly away from her.

"I don't need one, do you?" she answered softly.

He shook his head no, holding her gaze until she wiggled her hips beneath him.

Again she reached for him, positioning him to enter her. He moved softly against her, the pleasure of his touch sending currents of renewed desire through her. In a moment of animal hunger, she wrapped her legs around him to pull him deeply into her, welcoming him, lost in the passion and pleasure she felt at the feel of him inside her.

She writhed beneath him, eager to keep their bodies moving, feeling the touch of his skin moving against hers. Passion pounded the blood through her heart and her head, and she gasped in sweet agony as they found the tempo that bound their bodies together.

He moved with a powerfully sensual rhythm, until they reached the moment of ultimate pleasure together. He moaned low and called her name . . . over . . . and over. . . .

The turbulence of their passion flooded Celeste, clouding her mind with fragmented thoughts. She felt happily satisfied, but something clicked in her brain. Before she could grasp the fleeting thought, she felt the softness of Gabe's lips on her eye-lids. He covered her face with tender kisses, running his hands along her cheeks, massaging her temples, stroking her arms.

She abandoned her attempts to capture the disturbing thought and succumbed to the delicious feel of Gabe's hands as he rubbed and stroked every inch of her body.

Her eyes felt heavy and she fought to stay awake.

"We'll talk later," he whispered.

She concentrated on Gabe's voice, though it was barely audible, and so very far away.

Celeste sighed deeply and felt herself drift away into a sound, deep sleep.

Later that day, Kay walked into the living room where Celeste was curled up on the couch alone, munching her way through a giant bowl of buttered popcorn.

Celeste patted the space next to her on the sofa. "Want some?"

Kay reached for a handful of popcorn and sat down. "I want to know why Gabe's car was in front of your house when I woke up this morning. I'll have you know I kept three little girls from knocking on your door, which wasn't easy considering you had promised them blueberry pancakes."

"Oh, geez, I totally forgot —"

"That's okay, Jack's better so he met us at McDonald's for breakfast." Kay reached for another handful of popcorn before she continued. "So, tell me what's going on. You okay?"

Celeste shook her head. "Not really."

"I figured since you broke out the popcorn, things weren't so great. Remember how many bowls we went through every night when you first moved in here?"

Celeste stopped chewing, instantly recalling how she'd gorged herself on popcorn during the first few months after Wade's death. She shoved the bowl toward Kay. "I need help," she said, hoping she didn't sound too serious.

"Okay. You need questions?" Kay asked.

Celeste nodded. Kay had learned to fire questions at her to get her to open up, having quickly determined that she dreaded giving long monologues about her deepest feelings.

"Did Gabe spend the night?" Kay asked.

Celeste stared wide-eyed at her direct approach. "He dropped by early this morning just before dawn — looking really rumpled and stressed. He ended up helping me with a batch of cookies —"

"And things got a little hot in your kitchen?"

Celeste smiled. Kay was exactly what she needed right now. "Very hot. Afterwards, I fell asleep."

"And now you're filled with guilt and remorse at having slept with an engaged man," finished Kay.

"They canceled the wedding, actually."

"Well, yippy skippy. What are you so blue about, then?"

Celeste closed her eyes. What *was* bothering her so much? "I feel confused. It feels like I took Gabe from Jillian — I've been remembering all day about having done that with Wade and his girlfriend." She shook her head, exhaling loudly. "And Gabe is too much like Wade — into his all-important career, another heart attack waiting to happen."

"That's not fair, Celeste," Kay scolded.

Celeste sighed, hugging a pillow to her chest. "And still I feel attached, somehow, to . . ."

"Wade? Celeste, it's been over a year," Kay said softly. "Maybe all you need to do is spend some time sorting out your feelings, you think? I hate to say this, but divorce seems a whole lot easier than death, if you ask me. Being separated from someone by choice is a lot simpler than dealing with all those complicated emotions."

Celeste stared at Kay, absorbing her words.

"Maybe you just need to say good-bye to Wade in order to make room in your heart for someone else. Then decide if that someone is Gabe or not. It's not fair to keep him out of the race just because you think he's too much like what you lost." Kay patted Celeste's knee.

Celeste nodded, perplexed by her feelings toward her late husband, even though she was over the sadness, used to his absence.

"Want some advice?" Kay asked.

Celeste smiled. "And what does Dr. Kay have to say?"

"Go down to the beach. You know how much better we both think there — and don't come back until you've got it all figured out."

A sigh escaped from Celeste's lips. Kay was right. She gave her friend a hug. "Thanks, Kay. Now, get out of here. But, promise me you'll come looking for me if I'm not home by dark."

"Deal." Kay put the bowl of popcorn on the coffee table and quietly let herself out.

Sixteen

Celeste hugged her knees to her chest as she stared at the magnificent sunset. Bright pinks and oranges radiated in long, delicate streaks as the glowing red sun descended toward the liquid horizon. She leaned against the large, smooth boulder at the edge of the Coronado shoreline, the rock's hardness giving her a feeling of stability. The sand beneath her was soft, cradling her backside in a comforting way, connecting her to the earth. The tide had crested so she knew her position against the rock was safe, and the water lapped gently at the shore a couple of yards from her bare feet.

Celeste had walked the length of the beach back and forth for hours. It felt as if she had walked for miles when she finally allowed herself to stop and rest. She had replayed her entire married life in her mind, thanking Wade for everything he'd done for her, and forgiving him for his mistakes and shortcomings. Tears had come and gone. She'd acknowledged her anger and her fears, and identified and rejoiced in the good times they'd had.

Then she'd cut the thread and let him go. She said her final good-bye.

Celeste's thoughts were interrupted as a family of four walked into view. They stopped about twenty feet from her and spread a blanket onto the sand, where the two children immediately dropped down and wiggled out of their shoes. Then they scampered to the shore to wade in the water, bending over to look for shells and other sea treasures.

The sound of music from a radio drifted toward her and she was vaguely aware of the sound of her own voice from a Loveline commercial. It was the one they'd hardly been able to get through, she remembered, laughter filling the sound booth as they'd all tried to keep straight faces.

Brent's voice ended the commercial, explaining the continuation of the contest, and asking listeners to call in and vote for their favorites from that weekend's calls to the Loveline.

Then she heard the unmistakable sound of Gabe's voice.

"My Secret Valentine has no idea that I'm in love with her, but I think she'll know who she is if she's listening. All I can hope is that she'll trust her heart and recognize that we are meant to be together, which surprises me as much as it probably surprises her. My heart beats in time with yours, my love. Please give our love a chance."

"Oh," the woman on the blanket moaned, "that was the most romantic message I've ever heard. I sure hope that woman's listening."

Celeste closed her eyes, her heart thudding painfully. Of course he was talking about you, a little voice inside of her shouted.

She stood up and brushed the sand roughly off her backside. After a final look at the sunset, she turned away from the water and walked toward home, determined to get her life back to normal.

Celeste stretched her arms and yawned, then squinted at her bedside clock. Ten minutes until her alarm would go off. She'd slept like a rock — a deep, dreamless sleep, and she felt energized and exceptionally well-rested. Kay would say it was because she got laid, she thought, the sound of her friend's teasing voice ringing in her head.

She did feel wonderful. Rolling over, she pulled the extra pillow to her face to see if she could still smell Gabe. Breathing deeply, she captured his scent, and a tingle began between her thighs in instant response.

She and Gabe had made love in her bed. It still surprised her. Well, now what? she thought.

Now, no matter what, she knew she needed to see him. Talk to him.

Celeste kicked off her covers and sat up, a plan forming in her mind.

"Gabe, was that really you on the Loveline spot over the weekend?" Shelly poked her head into the booth and whispered her question to Gabe during a commercial break.

"Yup. And you have my permission to spread the news that Jillian and I have broken our engagement . . . *amicably.* Don't forget that part."

Shelly wrinkled her nose and crinkled her eyes at him. "For real?" she asked.

"It just wasn't the right thing for either of us . . . but I think you already knew that, didn't you?" Gabe smiled warmly returning his attention to the microphone.

When Shelly reached her desk, Jillian was standing in the lobby waiting for her.

Her hair was loose, skimming her shoulders in a casual flip, and she was dressed in a royal blue silk pantsuit with matching flats. She grinned at Shelly, who stood next to her desk, her mouth open in surprise.

"Hi, Shelly, what's up?"

"You look great — nice color on you, Jillian. I don't think I've ever seen you in pants."

"Did you talk to Gabe yet this morning?"

Shelly nodded as she sat down, reaching for her telephone headset.

"Then you've heard about . . . us, then?" Jillian asked.

"I'm so sorry —"

"Don't be, silly, we're both delighted that we figured it out before we went any further. By the way, I'm only here for the next hour. I'm going to take myself on a vacation for the next couple of weeks. Is my dad in?"

Shelly nodded as she buzzed the door for Jillian. "I saw him in the conference room earlier."

Jillian exhaled through her teeth. "He's gonna love this," she murmured, walking through the door, her head held high.

Celeste pulled into the parking lot of

KGLD, her stomach filled with fluttering butterflies. Her morning deliveries had gone quickly, though she'd had trouble keeping her mind on her work, missing more than a few exits as she drove from business to business, dropping off reorders of retail cookie gift baskets.

She put her hand on her chest, hoping to calm her fast-beating heart. What if Gabe's Loveline message had only been a spur-of-the-moment thing? What if he'd changed his mind? Paranoid thoughts kept Celeste frozen in her seat after she'd pulled into her usual parking space.

Shaking her head, Celeste turned off the ignition, leaving the radio on. The deep, calm sound of Gabe's voice filled her van.

"Another thanks to all you listeners out there who called in your Valentine messages to KGLD's Loveline over the last two weeks. Stay tuned for an announcement later today of the Grand Prize winner who all of you picked by calling in your votes for your favorite Loveline Valentine message. And now, let's start a no-talk thirty minute set of your favorite love songs from the fifties —"

Celeste snapped off the radio. She couldn't tell anything from Gabe's on-air voice. She'd just have to trust her instincts and believe he wanted to see her. With a sigh, she looked in the rearview mirror and tried to smooth her hair. It was wilder than ever, a reaction to the moisture in the air from a tropical storm that was approaching the San Diego area. Hair spray and gel only tamed her curls temporarily.

She wore a pale peach peasant style dress with a pastel-rainbow colored scarf tied around her waist. She had dressed and undressed three times before she was satisfied with the way she looked — feminine, but not too sexy, she'd thought, just in case.

With a deep breath, she climbed out of the van, retrieved a floral box from the back and walked into the lobby.

Shelly met her gaze and waved, continuing to talk to her caller, then pointed a thumb at the door and buzzed it open for her.

Celeste walked slowly down the hall, barely feeling the weight of her feet on the thickly carpeted floor. She felt lightheaded, dizzy from lack of oxygen. *Breathe,* she commanded herself.

Standing outside the on-air booth, Celeste moved into the doorway. Gabe's back was turned to her and he was straightening piles of papers and tapes on the console. She could hear the soft sounds of music coming from the speakers in the hallway.

Then Gabe froze, and turned around to face her.

"Looks like I've got an undelivered cookie bouquet here." Celeste hugged the box to her chest and waited. "Is it okay that I'm here?"

Gabe nodded. "Very okay."

"These are for you." Celeste stepped into the room and handed the white box to him. "Special delivery."

A red warning light blinked and Gabe rolled his eyes as he spun around to the console. He busied himself for a minute, setting up a commercial tape.

Celeste watched him work, fascinated with the speed in which he moved in the cramped space.

A Loveline commercial began playing — the sound of their two voices drifted into the room from the speakers in the hall.

Gabe grinned as he opened the box to see two dozen chocolate chip cookies on long green stems nestled in white tissue paper. He picked up a small white envelope and pulled out a gift card. He looked up at Celeste, staring at her wide-eyed face. She looked terrified, he thought, and beautiful. Her hair was wild and sexy as hell. She was wearing a delicate, pale peach dress, cinched at the waist with the scarf he had picked up off the floor of her closet the day before.

"Come here," he whispered, staring at her, the card still in his hand.

Slowly, Celeste walked toward him, the concern in her eyes softening with every step. He reached up to cup her chin, pulling her mouth towards his.

When their lips melted softly together, he could feel the heat instantly build within him. It was a soft kiss, a short kiss — just for reassurance.

She pulled away and gave him a dazzling smile. Gabe looked at the card, finally reading the words written there.

Dearest Gabe,
Looks like the secret's out about you and me.
I think I'm ready to follow my heart and give love another chance.
Celeste

Gabe read the words three times before he looked up and grinned at her. He brought his fingers to his lips, then leaned into the microphone.

"I'm going to end this especially marvelous Monday with an extra uninterrupted set of my own personal favorites. Be back tomorrow in the a.m."

Gabe snapped off the microphone and turned toward Celeste.

"Let's go somewhere," he said. "We've got a lot to talk about."

Celeste nodded, holding her hand toward him. "I know a great spot at the beach, close to home."

Epilogue

Celeste eased the Celestial Cookie van into a parking space in front of Anderson's music store, then reached behind her seat and grabbed a large box of cookies.

She stood on the sidewalk in front of the large display window, shading her eyes against the sun. She breathed a contented sigh as she admired the storefront.

Gabe had invested in a total remodel. The outside window was now shaded with a bright blue and white canvas awning, and a large sign hung there advertising acoustic folk music on Friday nights and Open Mike Night on Thursdays for local piano players.

Lettering on the window provided the Tuesday through Saturday store hours, plus rates for music lessons given by a growing list of local musicians and teachers. Celeste reached up to touch the gold letters of Mr. Anderson's name, glad she had helped convince him to continue giving lessons.

When Gabe had bought the store, he had also insisted on keeping the store's name, and he'd invited his old friend to be around as much as he wanted to be, providing inspiration to the youngsters that had made the music store a favorite hangout.

With a satisfied smile on her face, Celeste opened the door. The two rooms were now more formally divided since the remodel. One side still housed pianos and instruments for sale plus all the paraphernalia musicians required. Gabe had reorganized the space and almost doubled the inventory, adding new and used band instruments to support the local school music programs.

Celeste walked through the door, a bell tinkling her arrival, then she took an immediate right. The side that had once housed old LPs and turntables for sale had been fashioned into a casual gathering place. There, acoustic performances were held and visitors could take advantage of an eclectic listening library. Headphones and listening stations beckoned visitors to explore. Comfortable sofas and chairs encouraged musicians to congregate, and exchange ideas and advice.

Gabe had been thrilled when local teens

began to show up in the afternoons, playing guitar and piano and listening to the old blues and jazz standards he kept in the listening library.

Celeste opened the box of cookies and placed them on the counter next to the coffeepot. The afterschool crowd hadn't arrived yet. The room was peacefully still and yet, even empty, it seemed to be filled with an ambiance of creativity and harmony.

She loved what Gabe had done with the store and what the store had done for him. For one thing, it had awakened in Gabe a tremendous desire to coax his musical talent back to the surface. So, with Mr. Anderson's welcome input, he had managed to retain the store's practicality but he'd also been able to balance the retail side with an environment that encouraged musical exploration and creativity.

Heaven, she thought.

The sound of someone warming up on a piano in the retail side of the store drew Celeste's attention away from the cozy room. She walked back through the archway and saw Gabe seated at the old spinet piano that still sat at the end of the counter.

His fingers froze on the yellowed keys

when she approached. "Hi, gorgeous." He smiled a dimpled smile, his eyes sparkling with an untold secret.

"Hi, yourself. You working on something to play tonight?"

"You want to hear it?"

Celeste nodded, joining him on the piano bench, wrapping one arm around his waist.

Gabe began to play a dreamy-sounding waltz, the same song Mr. Anderson had played at that very piano, she realized, when she'd met him for the first time.

Celeste closed her eyes, floating with the melody, letting herself get lost in it. Then Gabe began to play a new part and Celeste's eyes snapped open, realizing he had finally finished the song he'd started in high school. She smiled as the song came to a wistful end with perfect, melodic closure.

"Very nice," she whispered. "Did you name it yet?"

"Celestial Serenade," Gabe whispered as he gathered her in his arms. "Well, Mrs. Freeman, you want to make out a little before the kids get here?"

Celeste smiled, reached her hands up until they were buried in Gabe's thick, now shoulder-length hair, and pulled him toward her for a congratulatory kiss.

About the Author

Janet Wellington has always believed in love and the pursuit of the perfect chocolate chip cookie recipe. She grew up spending wonderful childhood summers checking out ten books at a time each week from the neighborhood library. Her lifelong dream of becoming a published author is one of those special wishes that has come true with much hard work, perseverance, positive thinking, and a great deal of assistance from Romance Writers of America and the generosity of other writers.

Janet now teaches writing classes online and speaks at writing conferences all over the country. Her business, Wellington Word, offers writing services such as line-editing, proofing, and writing coaching. Read more about her at: www.janetwellington.com. Janet loves to hear from readers, and you can email her at mail@janetwellington.com or write to her at: PO Box 354, Florence, OR 97439.

P.S. And speaking of the perfect cookie, here is Brian Glasser's recipe for you to try:

2¼ cups all purpose flour
1 tsp. baking soda
1 tsp. salt
1 cup or two sticks of softened butter
¾ cup granulated sugar
¾ cup packed brown sugar
1 tsp. vanilla extract
2 eggs
2 cups chocolate chips
1 cup chopped nuts
2 cups peanut butter chips

Combine flour, baking soda, and salt in bowl. Beat the butter and the sugar (brown and granulated) and the vanilla in a large mixer bowl. Add the eggs, one at a time, beating well after each is added. Gradually beat in flour mixture. Stir in chocolate and peanut butter chips and nuts. Drop by rounded tablespoons onto ungreased baking sheets (for easier cleanup, use aluminum foil on sheets). Bake in 375 degree pre-heated oven for 9–11 minutes. Makes about 5 dozen or 60 cookies. Enjoy!

The employees of Thorndike Press hope you have enjoyed this Large Print book. All our Thorndike and Wheeler Large Print titles are designed for easy reading, and all our books are made to last. Other Thorndike Press Large Print books are available at your library, through selected bookstores, or directly from us.

For information about titles, please call:

(800) 223-1244

or visit our Web site at:

www.gale.com/thorndike
www.gale.com/wheeler

To share your comments, please write:

Publisher
Thorndike Press
295 Kennedy Memorial Drive
Waterville, ME   04901